WORKING STIFF

WORKING STIFF

The Cases of Dan Shamble, Zombie PI

Kevin J. Anderson

WFP

WordFire Press
Colorado Springs, Colorado

WORKING STIFF

ISBN: 978-1-61475-204-2

Cover painting by Jeff Herndon

Cover design by Kevin J. Anderson

Art Director Kevin J. Anderson

Book Design by RuneWright, LLC
www.RuneWright.com

Published by
WordFire Press, an imprint of
WordFire, Inc.
PO Box 1840
Monument CO 80132

Kevin J. Anderson & Rebecca Moesta, Publishers

WordFire Press Trade Paperback Edition March 2015
Printed in the USA
wordfirepress.com

Contents

Stakeout at the Vampire Circus

1

The circus is supposed to be fun, even a monster circus, but the experience turned sour when somebody tried to murder the vampire trapeze artist.

As a private detective, albeit a zombie, I investigate cases of all sorts in the Unnatural Quarter, applying my deductive skills and persistent determination (yes, the undead can be very persistent indeed). Some of my cases are admittedly strange; most are even stranger than that.

I'd been hired by a transvestite fortune-teller to find a stolen deck of magic cards, and he had sent me two free tickets to the circus. Gotta love the perks of the job. Not one to let an opportunity go to waste, I invited my girlfriend to accompany me; in many ways her detective skills are as good as my own.

Sheyenne is beautiful, blond, and intangible. I had started to fall in love with her when both of us were alive, and I still like having her around, despite the difficulties of an unnatural relationship—as a ghost, she can't physically touch me, and as a zombie I have my own limitations.

We showed our passes at the circus entrance gate and entered a whirlwind of colors, sounds, smells. Big tents, wild rides, popcorn, and cotton candy for the humans, more exotic treats for the unnaturals. One booth sold deep-fried artichoke hearts, while another sold deep-fried human hearts. Seeing me shamble by, a persistent vendor offered me a free sample of brains on a stick, but I politely declined.

I'm a well-preserved zombie and have never acquired a taste for brains. I've got my standards of behavior, not to mention personal hygiene. Given a little bit of care and effort, a zombie doesn't have to rot and fall apart, and I take pride in looking mostly human. Some people have even called me handsome—Sheyenne certainly does, but she's biased.

As Sheyenne flitted past the line of food stalls, her eyes were bright, her smile dazzling; I could imagine what she must have looked like as a little girl. I hadn't seen her this happy since she'd been poisoned to death.

Nearby, a muscular clay golem lifted a wooden mallet at the Test Your Strength game and slammed it down with such force that he not only rang the bell at the top of the pole, he split the mallet in half. A troll barker at the game muttered and handed the golem a pink plush bunny as a prize. The golem set the stuffed animal next to a pile of fuzzy prizes, paid another few coins, and took a fresh mallet to play the game again.

Many of the attendees were humans, attracted by the low prices of the human matinee; the nocturnal monsters would come out for the evening show. More than a decade had passed since the Big Uneasy, when all the legendary monsters came back to the world, and human society was finally realizing that unnaturals were people just like everyone else. Yes, some were ferocious and bloodthirsty—but so were some humans. Most monsters just wanted to live and let live (even though the definition of "living" had blurred).

Sheyenne saw crowds streaming toward the Big Top. "The lion tamer should be finishing, but the vampire trapeze artist is due to start. Do you think we could …"

I gave her my best smile. With stiff facial muscles, my "best smile" was only average, but even so I saved it for Sheyenne. "Sure, Spooky. We've got an hour before we're supposed to meet Zelda. Let's call it 'gathering background information.'"

"Or we could just call it part of the date," Sheyenne teased.

"That, too."

We followed other humans through the tent flaps. A pudgy twelve-year-old boy was harassing his sister, poking her arm incessantly, until he glanced at me and Sheyenne. I had pulled the fedora low, but it didn't entirely conceal the bullet hole in my forehead. When the pudgy kid gawked at the sight, his sister took advantage of the distraction and began poking him until their mother hurried them into the Big Top.

Inside, Sheyenne pointed to empty bleachers not far from the entrance. The thick canvas kept out direct sunlight, protecting the vampire performers and shrouding the interior in a pleasant nighttime gloom. My eyes adjusted quickly because gloom is a natural state for me. Always on the case, I remained alert. If I'd been more alert while I was still alive, I would be … well, still alive.

When I was a human private detective in the Quarter, Sheyenne's ghost had asked me to investigate her murder, which got me in trouble; I didn't even see the creep come up behind me in a dark alley, put a gun to the back of my head, and pull the trigger.

Under most circumstances, that would have put an end to my career, but you can't keep a good detective down. Thanks to the changed world, I came back from the dead, back on the case. Soon enough, I fell into my old routine, investigating mysteries wherever they might take me … even to the circus.

Sheyenne drifted to the nearest bleacher, and I climbed stiffly beside her. The spotlight shone down on a side ring, where a brown-furred werewolf in a scarlet vest—Calvin—cracked his bullwhip, snarling right back at a pair of snarling lions who failed to follow his commands. The thick-maned male cat growled, while the big female opened her mouth wide to show a yawn full of fangs. The lion tamer roared a response, cracked the whip again, and urged the big cats to do tricks, but they absolutely refused.

The lions flexed their claws, and the werewolf flexed his own in a show of dominance, but the lions weren't buying it. Just when it looked as if the fur was about to fly, a loud drumroll came from the center ring.

The spotlight swiveled away from the lion tamer to fall upon the ringmaster, a tall vampire with steel-gray hair. "Ladies and gentlemen, naturals and unnaturals of all ages—in the center ring, our main event!" He pointed upward, and the spotlight swung to the cavernous tent's rigging strung with high wires and a trapeze platform. A Baryshnikov look-alike stood on the platform, a gymnastic vampire in a silver lamé full-body leotard. He wore a medallion around his neck, a bright red ribbon with some kind of amulet, and a professional sneer.

"Bela, our vampire trapeze artist, master of the ropes—graceful, talented . . . a real swinger!" The ringmaster paused until the audience realized they were supposed to respond with polite laughter. Up on the platform, Bela lifted his chin, as if their applause was beneath him (and, technically speaking, it was, since the bleachers were far below).

"For his death-defying feat, Bela will perform without a safety net above *one hundred sharpened wooden stakes!*" The spotlight swung down to the floor of the ring, which was covered with a forest of pointy sticks, just waiting to perform impalement duties.

The suitably impressed audience gasped.

On the trapeze platform, Bela's haughty sneer was wide enough to show his fangs; I could see them even from my seat in the bleachers. The gold medallion at his neck glinted in the spotlight. Rolling his shoulders to loosen up, the vampire grasped the trapeze handle and lunged out into the open air. He seemed not to care a whit about the sharp wooden stakes as he swung across to the other side. At the apex of his arc, he swung back again, gaining speed. On the backswing, Bela spun around the trapeze bar, doing a loop. As he reached the apex once again, he released, did a quick somersault high in the air, and caught the bar as he dropped down.

The audience applauded. Werewolves in the bleachers howled their appreciation; some ghouls and less-well-preserved zombies let out long, low moans that sounded upbeat, considering. I shot a glance at Sheyenne, and judging by her delighted expression, she seemed to be enjoying herself.

Bela swung back, hanging on with one hand as he gave a dismissive wave to the audience. Vampires usually have fluid movements. I remembered that one vamp had tried out for the Olympic gymnastics team four years ago—and was promptly disqualified, though the Olympic judges could not articulate a valid reason. The vampire sued, and the matter was tied up in the courts until long past the conclusion of the Olympics. The vampire gymnast took the long view, however, as she would be just as spry and healthy in the next four-year cycle, and the next, and the next.

A big drumroll signaled Bela's finale. He swung back and forth one more time, pumping with his legs, increasing speed, and the bar soared up to the highest point yet. The vampire released his hold, flung himself into the air for another somersault, then a second, then a third as the empty trapeze swung in its clockwork arc, gliding back toward him, all perfectly choreographed.

As he dropped, Bela reached out. His fingertips brushed the bar—and missed. He flailed his hands in the air, trying to grab the trapeze, but the bar swung past out of reach, and gravity did its work. Bela tumbled toward the hundred sharp wooden stakes below.

Someone screamed. Even with my rigor-mortis-stiff knees, I lurched to my feet.

But at the last possible moment, the vampire's plummeting form transformed in the air. Mere inches above the deadly points, Bela turned into a bat, stretching and flapping his leathery wings. He flew away, the medallion still dangling from his little furry rodent neck. He alighted on the opposite trapeze platform, then transformed back into a vampire just in time to catch the returning trapeze. He held on, showing his pointed fangs in a superior grin, and took a deep bow. On cue, the band played a loud "Ta-da!"

After a stunned moment, the audience erupted in wild applause. Sheyenne was beaming enough to make her ectoplasm glow. Even I was smiling. "That was worth the price of admission," I said.

Sheyenne looked at me. "We didn't pay anything—we got free tickets."

"Then it's worth twice as much."

With the show over, the audience rose from the bleachers and filed toward the exit. "The cases don't solve themselves," I said to Sheyenne. "Let's go find that fortune-teller."

2

As Sheyenne and I walked along the midway in search of the fortune-teller's booth, we suddenly heard screams—not the joyful yelling of riders on a rickety roller coaster, but loud, terrified cries. Bona fide bloodcurdling shrieks. The screams of children.

I was moving before I even knew it, and Sheyenne flitted along beside me. Five children came running toward us, eyes wide enough to qualify the kids as amine cartoon characters. They yelled wordlessly, pelting past us.

They were running from a circus clown.

I had seen him on the circus posters: Fazio the Clown, grinning with a painted smile so wide he could have swallowed a bloody feast and not even left stains on his chin. His very appearance was supposed to be joyful and comforting, but I thought it looked diabolical—as it did to the kids, apparently.

Fazio implored, "Wait! I just want to make people laugh!"

Pursuing panicked children was not how *I* would have tried to make them laugh.

Panting, the clown stumbled up to us in his big floppy shoes. "I don't know what's wrong with kids today." His face was covered with white greasepaint, and he wore a bright red nose the size of a tennis ball. His bald cap was wrinkled over the top of his head, and shocks of pink hair stuck out in all directions. His teeth could have used whitening (a lot of it) and orthodontia (a lot of it). He held out a bicycle horn and honked it in my face. "Does that make you laugh?" Then he giggled, an edgy Renfield-catching-a-whole-handful-of-flies laugh.

"Sorry, not today," I said.

Glum, Fazio hung his head and shuffled off with his floppy shoes.

We found the booth of Zelda the fortune-teller, a rickety affair made of plywood and two-by-fours painted bright blue, festooned with crepe paper and a stenciled sign that said: FORTUNES TOLD: $5. But the price had been crossed out and reduced three successive times to the bargain rate of $1.

At the booth, a customer forked over a dollar bill, so we kept our distance, watching the fortune-teller in action. Zelda had told me to be discreet.

The customer was a potbellied man in plaid shorts and black socks. (And they say unnaturals look odd?) Zelda wore a curly wig of platinum-blond hair, eye shadow and blush that must have been purchased in bulk and applied with a trowel; the five o'clock shadow had come in a few hours early on the fortune-teller's cheeks. Gold hoop earrings, gold necklaces, and gold bangles accessorized a dress with a high neckline, but still showed planetary-sized bosomic curves, which were obviously just stuffing.

Zelda shuffled a well-worn deck of regular playing cards, then laid five cards face-up on the wooden tabletop in front of the customer. "The eight of clubs is a good sign—it shows you have worthy goals and are determined to achieve them." The supposedly female voice was falsetto and unconvincing.

He laid down another card. "The king of hearts indicates that you will be happy in romance, lucky in love."

"But when?" the man asked, plaintive.

"Unfortunately, the cards have no time stamp," Zelda said. "Now, the third one … ah, the three of spades! A very significant card. You are destined to have great financial success, but it may take a while, so be patient."

The man took hope from that. He looked at the last card. "And the jack of diamonds?"

Zelda shook her head. "That, unfortunately, is a minor card. It merely signifies that your breakfast won't satisfy you for long and you should seek refreshment from one of our fine food booths." The fortune-teller gathered the cards and restacked them in the deck as the customer bent down to pull up his black socks, which had slid lower on his ankles, then he walked off.

Taking our cue, Sheyenne and I stepped up to the fortune-teller. Zelda shuffled the deck, gave me a skeptical look. "I charge extra to determine the fate of the undead."

"We're not here for a reading, uh, ma'am. You hired us—I'm Dan Chambeaux, private investigator, and this is my associate Sheyenne."

Her voice dropped at least two octaves, and she lit a cigarette. "Of course, Mr. Chambeaux—thanks for stopping by." Zelda eyed my gaunt form, looked at my complexion, frowned at the bullet hole in my forehead. "Your business card didn't say you weren't alive."

"Those are old cards. I need to get them reprinted."

Sheyenne joined in. "We have references available upon request."

I got down to business. "I understand your magic fortune-telling deck has been misplaced? You need us to find it?"

"Not misplaced—*stolen.* I'm sure of it this time."

Some questions beg to be asked. "*This* time?"

"It's my second deck gone in six months! I thought I must have misplaced the first one—it happens in the circus, packing up, tearing down, day after day. But real magic fortune-telling decks are hard to come by, so I kept careful watch on the replacement cards. It was the last deck the supplier had in stock, and I couldn't afford another. But it's gone, too. Somebody stole it … somebody who's out to get me." He lowered his voice. "I predicted that, even without the cards!"

The customer is always right, as the saying goes; and also, the customer is sometimes paranoid. "We'll look into it, Mr., uh, Ms. Zelda."

"Aldo. My real name is Aldo Firkin. Zelda's just a stage name." He dabbed at the layers of peacock-colored eye shadow. "It's all an act."

"You don't say," I said. Sheyenne pretended to jab me with her spectral elbow, though I couldn't feel her touch. She sometimes has to remind me to show a proper professional attitude in front of the clients.

The fortune-teller frowned, plucking at the absurd dress. "You think I *want* to dress up like this? I'm not a natural-born transvestite, but I can't make a living otherwise. It's a stereotype we can't shake—nobody wants male fortune-tellers. What a sham! All these decades of fighting for equal rights, and I have to do this." He adjusted the ridiculous wig. "Now, about my stolen cards? I really need them back. I've been doing my best." With a burring rattle of laminated paper, Aldo/Zelda shuffled the regular playing cards. "But there's nothing magical about these. I'm just making it up. My other deck—now, those cards were *real,* the magic just barely starting to wear off."

His brow furrowed as he looked down at the old playing cards. "Oddly enough, my fortunes seem to be just as accurate with this ordinary deck. I must be really good at this." He tapped the deck, drew a card, looked at it, and smiled. "Ah, correctly predicted that one. Maybe there's real magic here!"

"Or maybe you're just telling people what they want to hear," I suggested.

Aldo grinned. "Ah, and that's the real magic, isn't it? Give cryptic fortunes and let the customer figure out the true meaning. 'You will lose something very valuable to you, but you will gain something unexpected.' That's one I told the fat lady a few months ago."

"Sounds like a bad horoscope," I said.

"Actually, it sounds like a *good* horoscope," Sheyenne said.

The gaunt vampire ringmaster walked by, still wearing his equestrian jacket; he kept to the awnings, shading his head with his black top hat to avoid the direct sunlight. Aldo waved. "Oscar! Come here—this is the private detective I was telling you about. Dan Chambeaux, meet Oscar Kowalski, ringmaster and circus owner."

The ringmaster gave a formal nod, and we exchanged a cold grip. "Dan Shamble?"

"Chambeaux," I corrected. "People always mispronounce my name. And I wouldn't expect a vampire to be named Oscar Kowalski. I'd think something more like … Bela."

Kowalski let out an annoyed snort. "Bela is a drama queen and a pain in the ass, but he does draw a crowd, and that's what it's all about." He lowered his voice. "I'm glad Aldo called you to look into the thefts. We've had a rash of them over the past two weeks." He shot a narrow-eyed glare at the transvestite fortune-teller. "But we need to be discreet."

Aldo sounded indignant. "He's a *private* detective, not a public one. And I couldn't wait any longer—I need my magic cards back."

"What other thefts?" Sheyenne pressed.

"Mostly minor items, low value," Kowalski said.

"My fortune-telling cards are extremely valuable!" Aldo insisted.

The ringmaster continued, "But it causes a lot of nuisance and unease. We like to think we're family here at the circus."

"I miss the Bearded Lady," Aldo muttered. "Harriet was like a mother to us all, really kept the circus tight-knit, like a family. Things were so much nicer before she went off to lead a semi-normal life of her own."

Kowalski shook his head. "We all miss Harriet, but there's not much call for everyday freaks after the Big Uneasy. People can see weirder creatures on any walk through the Quarter."

I got back to business. "We need to know what the other items are. All the clues should lead to the same suspect."

"I can get you a list—a long one," Aldo said, then considered. "But if you're investigating all of the thefts in the circus, then Oscar should pay your bill."

The ringmaster's shoulders drooped. "I'll pay *half* … provided Mr. Shamble—uh, Chambeaux—can help us all out. Most of the other items aren't worth much."

"If there's a thief running loose, maybe we should report it to Officer McGoohan?" Sheyenne suggested.

I explained, "I have a good friend on the police force. He'll take your problems seriously."

Kowalski cleared his throat. "That won't be necessary. We must count on your discretion, Mr. Chambeaux. People don't trust circus folk as it is, even here in the Unnatural Quarter, and I don't want to do anything to reinforce that stereotype. You probably don't like it when people consider all zombies to be brain-eating clods with speech impediments."

"Not at all," I said. "I work hard to stay well preserved."

Kowalski tipped his hat. "I hope you can resolve this quickly and quietly. The circus is your client."

"But find my magic cards first," Aldo insisted as he jotted down the list on a scrap of paper.

"If we find the thief, we should find all of the stolen items," I said.

Sheyenne and I read the list as we walked away. In addition to the magic fortune-telling cards (two sets, but I doubted we'd find the one he'd lost six months earlier), Aldo had listed a hammer (standard hardware store issue), glass milk bottle from one of the game booths, dagger from the knife thrower's act, three costume-jewelry necklaces from Annie the fat lady (hence a rope-length of jewelry), and a cold Reuben sandwich from a refrigerator in the Flag. I figured we could discount that last item.

We had no trouble finding the fat lady, mainly because she wasn't very mobile, but also because she was so large. In her open tent, Annie reclined on—and covered most of—a queen-sized bed. Plates mounded with chocolate chip cookies, brownies, and Danishes sat within reach of one hand; by the other side of the bed sat a tray of chicken wings and ribs. She had apparently been through several plates already, but despite the aftermath of her obviously enormous appetite, her face looked saggy. I didn't think the fat lady looked healthy at all, but since I'm undead, I'm not one to point fingers.

Annie's wide throat was round and somewhat tubular, like a pelican with a particular lucky catch of fish. She had permed gray hair and wire-rim glasses that made her look like the world's kindest, and largest, grandmother. An enormous floral muumuu extended all the way down to her ankles; sleeves covered the wrists where they met the gloves. Under her gigantic tent of a dress, her mounded belly stirred and squirmed in a disturbing way, as if her intestines were rearranging themselves before our eyes.

Annie gave us a twinkling smile. "Hello, dears! Come in and stare—that's what I'm here for. Would you like a cookie? I've got plenty." She extended the tray to us.

"No thanks, ma'am," Sheyenne said. "I'm ectoplasmic."

"And I'm on a low-carb diet," I added, even though it was just an excuse. My undead taste buds were no longer very discriminating, and Annie needed a constant stream of calories just to maintain her bulk. She consumed the rest of the cookies with methodical swiftness, as if it were her mission.

"We're from Chambeaux and Deyer Investigations, and we're here on a case." I set one of our business cards on the bedside table next to the chicken wings. "We've been hired to investigate certain items that have gone missing. If there's a circus thief, we'll catch him."

"A thief? Oh, my!" Annie held her hands to her face, licked a few crumbs from her fingers. "I refuse to believe members of my dear circus family are thieves." Her mounded stomach shifted and churned, and Annie let out an embarrassed giggle, placing her hands flat on her belly. "Just a bit of indigestion—it tends to get extreme in my case."

I held up Aldo's handwritten list. "According to this, you've lost several items of jewelry?"

"Oh, dear me, I may have misplaced a few cheap necklaces—I'm always doing that. When I manage to walk around, I can't see the ground, and if something falls … well, I just give it up for lost. I wouldn't call them *stolen.* The circus people are my family. I'm like a mother to them since Harriet's gone. Someone has to watch out for everyone."

I tipped my fedora. "If you think of anything, please let us know, ma'am. Any clue would help."

Leaving the fat lady's tent, we strolled along the midway, and soon Fazio the Clown buttonholed us again. "I saw you two talking with that fraud fortune-teller! He's a fake—a complete fake. I doubt he could predict *yesterday* if he had a newspaper in front of him."

If you had asked me before the Big Uneasy, I would have said that all fortune-telling was fake. Now, though, I'd seen plenty of evidence of functional spells. "He's at a disadvantage if he lost his magic cards."

"Not the cards—the sham costume. Him in his stupid wig and his clumsy makeup! It's an embarrassment. Makeup is no joke. I work hard on my appearance, greasepaint over every inch of exposed skin." He tugged at his shocks of pink hair, straightened the bald cap, then tweaked the bright red nose. "It's a beautiful design, the perfect clown face—I've even got it trademarked. But Zelda, or Aldo, or whoever or whatever the name is, does it just to make a buck. It cheapens the art of face painting."

"And why do you paint your face?" Sheyenne asked.

"For a greater purpose, of course—to get a laugh."

Or a scream, I thought, remembering the terrified children.

"We're investigating a rash of burglaries, not makeup techniques," I said. "Any comments about his missing deck of fortune-telling cards?"

"I don't know anything about the first one he lost, and not the second one either." He snorted, then stormed off. "You should be investigating Aldo. His eye shadow is a crime!"

3

After gathering as much information as we could, Sheyenne and I returned to the Chambeaux & Deyer offices in the seedy, run-down section of the Unnatural Quarter (I realize that's not very specific).

Sheyenne began compiling a list of circus suspects and digging up dirt on them. She's good at uncovering details, whether they be sordid details, suspicious details, or just plain bookkeeping details.

A large part of my job is time management. Real life as an undead private investigator isn't like a TV detective show, where the PI works on one mystery at a time and solves it without other clients getting in the way. In addition to investigating stolen items at the vampire circus, I had several active cases.

My partner, Robin Deyer, came out to brief me on the legal battles she had fought during the day. As a lawyer, Robin makes sure that downtrodden and underrepresented monsters get a fair shot in the legal system. She's a young African American, as pretty as she is determined—and she is extremely determined. Her eyes had a faraway, preoccupied look because case subtleties ran through her head at all times.

I had taken her under my wing back when I was a human private detective. We shared office space, offered assistance on each other's cases, and enjoyed working together. After my murder, I think Robin was hit even harder by my death than I was. When I came back from the grave, she welcomed me with open arms (after she got over the shock and uneasiness). She made a special point to treat me just as she'd always done, and we quickly got back to our usual routine.

"Any word on the gargoyle case?" I asked.

For several weeks Robin had represented a gargoyle who was suing the Notre Dame cathedral for unauthorized use of his likeness. Comparing the gargoyle himself with photographs of several specific stone figures on the ancient cathedral, the resemblance was undeniable.

Her expression tightened. "I think we're going to lose that one. There seems to be an unbreakable statute of limitations clause in church law. Today, I'm neck-deep in that unnatural voting rights case."

Robin was tilting at a different windmill, challenging voter restrictions recently put in place for the sole purpose of denying unnaturals the right to vote. (No one seemed to remember that in some corrupt cities, dead people had done more than their share of voting over the years....) Both political parties insisted that the proposed voter suppression rules against unnaturals were disenfranchising their constituents, although neither side had been able to prove that unnaturals leaned toward any particular affiliation, as a rule.

After Robin described a brief she had filed and her court appearance schedule for the week, I told her about the vampire circus and headed to my office to take care of my own work. "I think I can wrap up the Amontillado case this afternoon."

"Good," Sheyenne called from the receptionist's desk. "We need to send them a bill."

Robin cautioned, "The outcome wasn't what the client expected. Maybe we should offer a discount—"

Sheyenne cut right in. "The client is a client, and a fee is a fee." If Robin had her way, she would do all cases pro bono, and Sheyenne often had to remind her about the facts of business. Even though I was undead and Sheyenne was a ghost, *Robin* still needed to eat, and we all had to pay the rent on the office space.

I suggested a compromise. "Give the client a coupon for his next case with us. We did solve the mystery, which is what he hired us to do."

A wealthy man had asked me to track down a very rare cask of Amontillado, more than a century and a half old, and I found the cask behind a brick wall, along with an animated skeleton that had been manacled there. In the years since the Big Uneasy, the skeleton had managed to break loose from one manacle by detaching his entire bony hand. With his wrist released, he was able to reach the cask, work the bung loose, and pour the extremely expensive sherry down his throat. Of course, since he had no throat, the rare Amontillado spilled all over the vault floor and dried up. When I found the very expensive and very empty cask I'd been hired to track down, the skeleton laughed and laughed at the joke, saying in a rattling voice, "I drank it all, I drank it all!"

Now I sat at my desk and wrote up the report, reducing the total number of hours billed on the case just to make Robin happy, and to make me feel better as well; Sheyenne didn't need to know.

It was full-dark outside by the time Sheyenne flitted through my closed office door. She carried a stack of papers, which could not spectrally pass through the barrier, so they fluttered to the floor outside. With an impatient frown, she flitted back out, picked up the papers, and opened the door to enter via the normal way.

"I ran down the usual suspects at the circus. Some very interesting background material."

I took the papers. "Anything suspicious?"

She arched her eyebrows. "Naturals and unnaturals all working for a traveling circus run by a vampire—isn't that suspicious enough?"

"I was hoping for something more specific."

"So many aliases, stage names, plenty of skeletons in the closet—and not like the one you found with your cask of Amontillado." She grinned at me.

"Speaking of that ..." I handed her the bill and final report, which pleased her very much.

She continued with her summary, "First off, Oscar Kowalski is not a very talented businessman. He's filed for bankruptcy twice since the Big Uneasy, barely scraped through, and seems to be in rocky circumstances right now."

I said, "I don't see how stealing a deck of fortune-teller cards, costume jewelry, and a cold Reuben sandwich would help his financial situation."

"Probably not." Sheyenne glanced down at her papers again. "Checking back along the circus route over the years, I found that two goblin roustabouts were arrested for petty theft, but they escaped and disappeared. Young twins. Their juvenile records should have been sealed, but Robin pried them loose because the law is still murky."

"Robin used a murky law to her own advantage?" I asked. "Good for her."

Sheyenne blew an imaginary breath through her lips. "The goblins were over eighteen years old—adults according to the letter of the law—but goblins live a long time, and those twins are still adolescents as far as *goblins* go. Still, nobody's bothered to change the law, so we got the arrest records. Not that it does us much good, if the twins are no longer with the circus."

Robin would probably decide to challenge that law, now that she'd noticed the injustice.

"What else?" I asked.

"Aldo—or should we call him Zelda?—is late on his child support, and his ex-wife is trying to track him down." She checked off items on her list. "Fazio got arrested for drunk driving in his clown car, but that was never prosecuted. Oh, and his clown license has expired."

I frowned. "I didn't know there was such a thing as a clown license. I find that very suspicious."

Sheyenne blinked her blue eyes at me. "More suspicious than all the other things?"

"He's a clown. I'm always suspicious of clowns."

4

With the information Sheyenne had uncovered about the circus personnel, I went back to the midway early enough to catch the nighttime monster matinee. While unnatural crowds started to gather inside the Big Top for Bela's performance, I stopped by Oscar Kowalski's office trailer just outside the main tent. I wanted to ask him about bankruptcy filings, late child-support payments, Fazio's expired clown license, and anything else that came to mind. Instead, I stumbled into another crisis.

"I refuse, Oscar!" Bela cried with an exaggerated and obviously fake Transylvanian accent. He raised his chin with an imperious air and flared the nostrils on his beak-like nose. "You must cancel the show. I can't perform under these circumstances—it is impossible!"

"Nothing's impossible, Bela." Kowalski sounded long-suffering and annoyed. He sat at his desk with an open, and messily scribbled ledger. "Nobody's canceling the show. You *can* go on, and you *will* go on."

"But it's been stolen!" Bela clutched at his throat, where I noticed the gold medallion was missing. (The far-too-clingy silver lamé bodysuit had previously demanded most of my attention.) "It's my Air Commander medal, given to me for being a Flying Ace in World War Two—or World War One, I forget which. If I don't wear the medal, then I won't have the confidence to transform into a bat at the climax of my show."

I interrupted, startling them. "You need a magic talisman to change into a bat?"

"Have you ever tried it?" Bela snapped, then whirled on Kowalski. "Have *you?* Most vampires are incapable. It requires the utmost concentration. My Air Commander medal is the perfect focusing aid."

"So it's like Dumbo's magic feather?" I said. "Without it, you wouldn't have the self-confidence to fly?"

Bela raised himself up, looked down his nose at me, and said with withering sarcasm, "Yes, exactly like that." He sniffed.

"It's all in his head," Kowalski explained to me. "Nothing magical whatsoever. The medallion's just a piece of junk."

"It is part of my act! I feel naked without it."

Again, I had trouble tearing my attention from the excessively form-fitting lamé bodysuit.

The ringmaster looked at his watch, closed his ledger with finality. "Sorry, Bela, but the show must go on. So follow that advice—*go on!*"

In a huff, the vampire trapeze artist strutted out of the admin trailer.

With a flicker of relief on his face, Kowalski turned to me. "Every week he's got some other excuse, imagines he's been cursed whenever he passes gas, threatens to quit the circus, but I doubt any rival show would have him."

"Are there other monster circuses?" I hadn't heard of any.

"No. Hence, my point. And I admit it takes a lot of concentration to turn into a bat, especially on the fly, but he doesn't have to be such an ass about it." He brushed down his jacket, looked at the watch again. "Now, I didn't expect to see you back so soon, Mr. Chambeaux. Come up with answers yet?"

"Even better—I've got a lot more questions."

"How is that better?"

"That means I'm making progress."

Kowalski stood from his desk. He looked tired as he reached for his top hat. "I can't talk with you at the moment. The show must go on for me, too, and if there's any unreasonable delay in the performance the lions start complaining."

"Don't you mean the lion tamer?" I asked.

"No, Calvin's easy to deal with, but the lions want their treats, and they can get quite demanding." He showed me out of the trailer and locked the door behind us.

With the audience crowded in the Big Top for the monster matinee, the midway was quiet and dark. I decided to lurk and snoop, two things for which a zombie detective is eminently qualified.

Since the Air Commander medal was the latest stolen item, I made my way to Bela's darkened tent. Though he considered himself the star of the circus, the vampire's mobile domicile wasn't much more than a place to shelter his coffin when he needed some quiet time—wide open and not secure. If Bela had gone to ground to take a nap, someone could easily have snatched his medal from the nightstand and run off with it.

I walked around outside Bela's tent, senses alert and scanning the ground for any unusual clues … such as that playing card lying face-up on the ground not far from the tent.

It was the jack of diamonds, the same card that predicted a person would be hungry soon after breakfast. I guessed it came from Zelda's deck.

I kept plodding along, scanning from side to side. The circus seemed eerily empty, filled with shadows. I heard the audience cheer in the Big Top; Calvin must be in the middle of his act.

Spotting something ahead, I bent over to pick up another playing card, the six of hearts. With two dropped playing cards making a dotted line that led from Bela's recently burgled tent toward the general direction of Zelda/Aldo's trailer, I knew how to connect the dots.

As I approached the trailer, I heard raised voices, an argument in full swing. Aldo was shouting, so upset that he still sounded high-pitched and falsetto, and not in an attempt to maintain his transvestite identity. "What did you want with my magic cards anyway? It wasn't enough for you to steal my fortune-telling deck, so you had to steal my playing cards, too? And my makeup kit? You're trying to ruin me!" He had his wig in his hand, and a smear of cold cream had removed only the first few layers of eye shadow.

Fazio was still in full clown makeup, his bright red nose planted in the middle of his white-painted face, his pink hair sticking out in all directions. "You have nothing I'd even want to steal—certainly not your amateur makeup kit! You are a fake and a disgrace!"

Before they could come to blows, I interrupted, holding up the two playing cards. "Are these from the deck? I found them on the ground near Bela's tent—there's been another robbery."

Aldo grabbed the playing cards, as if he could make a good start with only two of the fifty-two. "Yes, there has—my cards and my makeup kit."

Fazio asked, "What other robbery?"

"Someone took Bela's Air Commander medal right before his trapeze act."

"Bela never goes anywhere without that gaudy thing." Aldo crossed his arms over his too-obviously padded chest, then turned to the clown. "Why would you steal the poor vamp's Air Commander medal?"

"I *didn't* steal it! And I didn't steal your damn cards, either! Or your makeup kit. I am a completely honest, law-abiding citizen."

"Then what about my Reuben sandwich?" Aldo demanded. Fazio hesitated just long enough for the fortune-teller to pounce. "I knew it—you took my sandwich!"

"Those may be two unrelated cases," I said. "And, Fazio, you're not off my list of suspects—I know you've been keeping secrets."

The circus clown seemed to turn even whiter than his greasepaint. "You … know my secret?"

"Your clown license is expired, and that's enough to make me suspicious," I said, deciding not to bring up the clown-car drunk driving incident. "I can bring in the real police at any time, but for now I'll keep looking."

I stalked off among the dark trailers and tents. I hoped I could find the Air Commander medal in time to take it to the vampire trapeze artist before his act, just to give him a psychological boost. The crowd in the Big Top continued to cheer the lion tamer's show.

I paused at Annie's tent. Since the tent flaps were open, I looked in. The fat lady was inside, lying on her bed, and appeared to be asleep, covered by a mounded blanket. She looked like a mountain range under the comforters. More plates piled with cookies, brownies, ribs, and wings remained within easy reach; someone must replenish them all day long. I left her to rest.

I circled around, trying to keep an open mind but ready to find Fazio responsible (okay, I admit, I was guilty of clown profiling). There, outside the front of his tent, I found the red ribbon and gold disk—Bela's Air Commander medal, just lying on the ground. Not only was the circus thief persistent and random, he was also clumsy. Why steal things, then drop them all over the place like a cat losing interest in a mouse?

In the Big Top, the crowd cheered and applauded as Calvin finished his show. I grabbed the medal, deciding to confront the clown later. At the moment I had to get the Air Commander medal back to the vampire trapeze artist before he started his act.

I expected to feel a tingle of magic; if the Air Commander medal were really a spell-impregnated amulet, I should have been able to sense the power even with my numb fingers. Then the "gold" disk rotated as I dangled the ribbon, revealing *Made in China* stamped on the back; I suspected the disk itself was nothing more than coated tin.

But Bela somehow had it in his head that he needed this thing for his bat transformation, so I might as well be of service.

I raced to the Big Top at the best speed I could manage—joints and muscles tend to stiffen up postmortem, so it's a good thing I keep myself in shape. So many spectators were milling at the main tent opening—mummies, werewolves, ghouls, vampires, a very tall ogre—that I couldn't get inside, so I ran around to the side by Oscar Kowalski's office trailer. I pushed my way through a smaller stage entrance, holding up the medal. "Wait—I have to get this to Bela before he starts!"

But the ringmaster had already announced the performance, and the crowd drowned out my voice. Spotlights shone on Bela, high up on his trapeze platform, and the audience gave suitable gasps as the light swung down to illuminate the hundred sharpened stakes.

For all his prima donna behavior, Bela was a true showman. Even without the not-so-magic medal around his neck, he showed no sign of nervousness as he grabbed the trapeze and swung out over the yawning gap. As Bela began his act, Kowalski withdrew to the side of the tent, where he saw me holding the red-ribboned amulet. "I found it," I said, "but too late."

The ringmaster gave a snort. "He doesn't need the thing. It's all in his head, and I can't let him make excuses. The show must go on."

Above, Bela did a beautiful somersault loop, then caught the trapeze bar again.

"His ego needs to be taken down a notch anyway. He demanded a big pay raise. Does he think the circus is actually making any money? We're holding on by a spiderweb here."

I lowered my voice. "I know about the bankruptcies, Mr. Kowalski."

The ringmaster frowned. "So then you know I can't pay Bela anymore, but I can't have him leave, either. If he refused to do the show tonight, and I had to refund all these tickets …" He gestured to the audience. "I might as well bury myself six feet under without a book to read."

Bela swung back and forth on the trapeze, increasing his momentum and height as he set up for the climax of the show.

Kowalski looked up. "The fumble is all part of the act, you know. He better not chicken out tonight."

At the apex of the swing, Bela flipped himself into the air, spun three somersaults, then reached out to catch the returning bar, fumbled and missed—just as I had seen him do that afternoon. Bela wore a panicked look, his arms outstretched as he plummeted toward the pointy wooden stakes.

The audience gasped. A necromancer screamed in a high, womanish voice. Kowalski and I waited for Bela to transform into a bat.

And waited.

He flailed and thrashed in real panic. In the last instant, Bela squeezed his eyes shut, either in a last-ditch attempt to concentrate or to avoid seeing so many sharp wooden tips. And then he slammed into them. Since he'd been falling spread-eagled, Bela managed to impale himself on a goodly number of the one hundred stakes.

Kowalski gaped. The monsters in the audience screamed; some chuckled, thinking it was part of the show. But when Bela sizzled and fumed, his body boiling and flesh sloughing away to leave only a skeleton that crumbled to dust, people began running out of the Big Top. A few stayed and applauded.

"I have to manage this crowd!" Kowalski said as he bolted away from me. "The show's over—you saw it finish. Nobody's getting refunds."

Disgusted, I held up the Air Commander medal and called after him. "I found this by Fazio's tent—and I bet he also stole Aldo's deck of fortune-telling cards."

Then I had another thought, realizing that the uproar would let Fazio know that Bela was dead—and the clown *knew* he was responsible. If the amulet truly had no magic, I didn't know whether this counted technically as murder, but at the very least he had caused a deadly accident, messing with the vampire trapeze artist's head before a dangerous act. Fazio had some explaining to do, and I had to stop him before he fled the circus.

I pulled out my cell phone and called Officer Toby McGoohan, commonly called McGoo (by me, at least), and told him to roll the squad cars, that we had a death at the circus and a possible murderer to arrest. McGoo likes to hear things like that. He's my BHF—my best human friend—and we've helped each other on many cases. I knew I could count on him now.

First, though, I had to prevent the escape of a deadly circus clown.

5

I expected to find Fazio at his tent, stuffing valuables into a hobo sack so he could run far from the Quarter. That's what *I* would do if I were a killer clown cat burglar responsible for the death of a vampire trapeze artist.

I did find Fazio in his tent, but he wasn't packing up to leave. Instead he was wailing, outraged. "They stole my nose! The little bastards stole *my nose!*"

The clown whirled to face me, and I saw that the big red nose was indeed gone from the middle of his face. More shocking, though: The fake nose wasn't the only thing missing. Fazio's *real* nose was gone, leaving a cavernous empty sinus socket draped with a few shreds of rotted flesh. The makeup had been smudged around his eyes, and I could see the sunken hollow look, the grayish tone to his unpainted skin.

"You're a *zombie!*" I cried, demonstrating my detective abilities.

"Not just a zombie," Fazio insisted. "A clown, too. That's my true calling in life—and afterlife."

A zombie clown, I thought. Now *that's* scary.

Fazio moaned, covering the nose hole in the middle of his face. "All I ever wanted was to make people laugh." Then he looked up at me. "Why are *you* so surprised? You're undead, and you came back to keep solving cases. Why can't I still be a clown just because I'm a zombie? Maybe that's why I rose up in the first place—to make people laugh."

Actually, he wasn't making anyone laugh that I could tell, but I decided not to argue with him.

He touched his cheeks. "Put on enough greasepaint and a wig, no one can tell the difference. I still do my job." A wave of anger passed through him again. "And those little goblin bastards stole my nose! I thought we were done with them for good! Last time they were here, the twins stole everything that wasn't superglued down." He let out a huff. "In fact, we *tried* supergluing everything down … which did prevent the thefts, but kept us from using the items at all. Bad idea. And then they stole the tube of superglue."

"Which way did they go?" I heard sirens wailing in the distance. McGoo responded quickly, especially when he knew he'd have a nice arrest on his record without having to do the footwork.

The clown sniffled again—which came out as a loud hooting sound without his nose—and pointed out the tent. "They grabbed the nose off my face and ran that way. Somebody must be hiding them."

"What would they do with a clown nose?" I asked. "Can you sell it on an auction site somewhere?"

"They don't *do* anything with what they steal—they just steal it. It's an illness. That's why you find so many things just lying around on the ground."

I bolted out of Fazio's tent, hoping to intercept the kleptomaniac goblins. The circus midway was full of attendees streaming toward the exits, chattering about Bela's spectacular (and, most agreed, *entertaining*) death. Some unnaturals still insisted it was part of the show and were trying to figure out how the trick was done.

Then I spotted another playing card lying on the ground and a necklace a few steps beyond that, then a baseball cap, and an eye patch. This was like a scavenger hunt. All of the breadcrumbs were heading toward the fat lady's tent.

I heard a scuffle and a squeal, and I put on a burst of speed; zombies can move quickly in emergencies, or when they're especially hungry. "Over here!" I yelled, hoping someone else would come running. I already knew Fazio was sounding the alarm among his circus friends, who were already alarmed after the death of the vampire trapeze artist (or maybe just because of the approaching police sirens).

The flaps of the fat lady's tent were down, but I yanked them open. I saw Annie struggling with her enormous dress, pulling down the fabric folds to cover her body—and the dress itself, or something inside it, was fighting back.

"Quickly, my dears, quickly!" When she saw me, a look of horror crossed her face (I often get that reaction). She did not look like a sweet granny now; her whole face was much skinnier, as if someone had deflated her. Annie still had many chins, but they hung like wattles around her neck.

As she struggled and thrashed with her recalcitrant dress, the fabric tore, and a goblin's smooth, ugly head poked out. The second young goblin also squirmed and broke free, ripping the dress to shreds as they both escaped from their unorthodox hiding place. Inside the tentlike flower-print fabric, they left behind a rather scrawny-looking Annie in a one-piece bathing suit. The goblins hissed and snapped, annoyed to be exposed.

Goblins are like small gray-skinned elves ... if those elves happened to be born from a mother saturated with toxic waste and poisonous thoughts. Their huge mouths were filled with needle-like teeth, and their glowing eyes could have been used as a plumber's utility light. As the goblin twins tried to scramble away, Annie wrapped her arms around them and pulled the creatures close to her in a motherly embrace.

There was hardly anything to Annie now. With all her loose skin, she looked as if she was wasting away, despite the numerous plates of ribs, cookies, etc., she consumed every day. Then I realized that if she had been hiding the kleptomaniac creatures, they might have eaten much of the food.

The fat lady's eyes were wide, her expression desperate. "You can't take my boys!" She yanked the goblins closer, practically smothering them. "I was trying to protect them, and they helped me when I needed it most! They're so sweet." She held out her hand, and one of the goblins tried to bite it. Annie giggled.

More shouts came from outside the tent. Fazio, the now-noseless clown, staggered in, accompanied by Aldo, who'd thrown on his wig while he ran, as well as the werewolf lion tamer, who still held his bullwhip, ready to use it.

The vampire ringmaster barged in right behind them, distraught. "The police are coming. What the—" He stopped when he saw the goblins. "What the hell are those two doing here? With all the arrest warrants—"

As the kleptomaniac goblin twins tried to bolt, Calvin cracked his bullwhip, and they skittered back into Annie's protective embrace.

"I won't turn them out into the cold," she said with a sniffle. "They're just misunderstood. They stole things, but they didn't mean anything bad by it."

"Nothing bad?" Kowalski cried. "They stole Bela's Air Commander medal. Without it, he didn't think he could turn into a bat—and now he's dead!"

Annie was disturbed by this. "But he started out dead."

"I mean he's really dead now!"

"Well, I'm sure they're very sorry," Annie insisted.

"The medallion was fake." I held it up so everyone could see the words *Made in China* stamped on the back. "No intrinsic magic."

Annie sounded defensive. "There—no harm done."

The clown and the fortune-teller looked at the strangely emaciated form of the fat lady. Aldo said, "What happened to you? You used to be so … so …"

"Fat," she answered.

"I was about to say *substantial*." Then Aldo remembered his priorities. "And what happened to my fortune-telling cards?"

"I lost weight, thanks to your magic cards." She sniffed, sounding glum. "When Harriet left the circus, I wanted to be in better shape to mother you all. It's quite a job! I wanted to be healthy, go on a diet, so I signed up for a guaranteed Gypsy weight-loss routine. Mean Cuisine. I lost four hundred pounds—and now I can't stop!"

Aldo scratched his wig, which was already askew. "What did my fortune-telling deck have to do with it?"

"I needed your cards, ones with real magic, and that's why I took your deck six months ago." She sniffed and made an excuse. "Well, you did leave them lying around a lot." When the fortune-teller glared at her, she turned away. "I just had to have two specific cards, the fat lady and the skeleton. I superglued the cards together, read the spell from the Gypsy diet book, and *this* fat lady started to look more like a skeleton. Worked like a charm!"

"Uh, it *was* a charm," I pointed out.

"But because of the superglue, I couldn't separate the cards again. Impossible to break the spell. And I realized I was going to lose my livelihood! Being a fat lady is all I am … and believe me, there was a lot of me." She pulled at the excessive folds of her torn dress. "Everybody loved me when I was a fat lady. Everyone wanted to hug me, lose themselves in my expansive … everything. I needed another fortune-telling deck, a fresh skeleton card and a fat lady card, so I could break the magic."

"So you stole my other deck, too!" Aldo said.

"The goblin boys did." Annie sounded ashamed. "You were much more careful after losing the first one, and I wasn't exactly nimble enough to slip into your trailer unnoticed. The boys came back to the circus, looking for shelter and hoping to hide from the police, and I just asked them to do me that one favor. Unfortunately, once they got started …"

Officer McGoohan and four uniformed cops charged into the tent, all trying to fit through the open flap at once, as if they were performing their own circus clown act. Fortunately, because it was designed for a fat lady, the tent opening was double-wide.

McGoo's a rough, tough cop who gets himself in trouble more often than the criminals do, but he and I have gotten each other *out* of trouble enough times, too. "Shamble, tell me what's going on here."

I rattled off a quick summary. "Fat lady hiding kleptomaniac goblins in her dress, a vampire trapeze artist accidentally murdered because he couldn't change into a bat, deck of magic fortune-telling cards stolen—among other things."

McGoo nodded. "Oh, another one of those cases."

The goblins tried to bolt as the policemen rounded them up, and Calvin used his whip with great enthusiasm as well as precision. Even after the goblin thieves were handcuffed, they snapped with their needle-like teeth, trying to bite the hands that arrested them. Fortunately, among his other useful defensive items, McGoo kept a roll of duct tape on his belt, with which he secured the criminal goblins' mouths.

"Oh, my poor dears," Annie wailed. "They just need some love and understanding."

"They need a little time behind bars," I said. "Or at least doing community service." All in all, I doubted the stolen items added up to more than a misdemeanor.

"There are other arrest warrants for those two." McGoo was shaking his head. "And the fat lady was aiding and abetting."

"For petty theft," Kowalski said, troubled. "Bela might disagree, but he never liked to accept blame for anything. He did sign a waiver acknowledging the inherent risk in performing death-defying feats."

Kowalski stood next to Annie. "The circus is like family, and Annie is part of it. We're not pressing charges against her, and we'll return all the stolen items to their rightful owners."

"Except for my magic deck," Aldo grumbled.

"I can track down another one," I said. "Part of my services."

"And my Reuben sandwich."

"Can't help you there...."

Without asking permission, the clown and the fortune-teller worked together—a victory in itself—to open the trunks in the back of Annie's tent, moving aside the plates piled with cookies and gnawed rib bones. Fazio lifted out a bright red ball. "Here's my nose!"

Digging deeper, they also found what was left of the deck of magic fortune-telling cards. Aldo was dismayed as he counted through them to find the skeleton and fat lady cards torn in half, by which Annie had apparently broken the weight-loss spell; other cards were missing as well, probably strewn on the ground somewhere along the midway.

The former fat lady wept, still clutching at straws. "Maybe if everything's returned, there won't be any charges filed?"

"Suit yourselves." McGoo shook his head as the cops wrestled the still-squirming goblins out of the tent. "Those boys have already gotten themselves into enough trouble, more than just robbing circus folk. They'll probably serve a year in juvie, maybe get out early for good behavior. Or maybe not."

"Yes, they are quite a handful," the fat lady said. "Even I have to admit that." Looking longingly after the wayward goblins, Annie drew a deep shuddering breath, then turned to Oscar Kowalski. "I don't suppose the circus has any use for a *skinny* lady? At least until I fill out a little bit? The spell is broken, and I'm gaining weight again ... and it'll be even faster when the twins don't eat most of my food."

The ringmaster thought long and hard. "I could use someone who understands the circus—and business. I'm no good at handling the day-to-day paperwork, the administration, managing the employees. I'm a showman, not an accountant." He propped himself up, snatched off his top hat. "I never was much good at the business side of things. You'd think a vampire circus would *want* to be in the red."

Annie finally brightened. "I can help. I can be like a mother to everyone. And if I manage the money, it'll be like giving everybody an allowance!"

Fazio had reapplied his nose, although his makeup remained smeared. He looked at the remaining platters of food. "Annie, you wouldn't happen to have a banana-cream pie I could smash into someone's face? Just for the gag?"

"Sorry, dear, I only have cookies."

The zombie clown threw cookies at Calvin, but nobody laughed. Rather, the werewolf lion tamer caught them and munched politely.

Aldo came up to me, smiling. "Thank you for everything, Mr. Chambeaux. You did track down the cards, and the thieves. And if you can find a replacement deck ..." He held out his abbreviated deck of magic cards, shuffled them, and extended the pile to me. "Pick a card, any card."

I did, looked at it myself, then slid it back into the deck. "No, thanks."

Aldo frowned. "Don't you want to know your future?"

"I'm a detective," I said. "I'd rather figure it out for myself."

ROAD KILL

1

It's never a good thing to wake up in a coffin, unless you're a vampire—and I'm definitely not a vampire. I'm an entirely different sort of undead.

Now, vampires *belong* in coffins; they actually find them comfortable. Vamps go there regularly to get their sleep. I've even known several who kept everyday coffins and vacation coffins (fitted with tropical interior décor). Some are just stripped-down pine boxes, while others are luxury models rigged with stereo systems for music or audiobooks. Some coffins even have tingly massage fingers on the bottom.

The coffin I woke up in wasn't one of those types, and I sure as hell didn't belong here.

I'm a zombie, and zombies aren't so picky about where they rest. Sure, coffins will do just fine, but once we've clawed our way out of the grave, we don't need to sleep often, and when we do we're okay with sleeping on a sofa, or even just propped up in a corner somewhere. It doesn't really matter.

But I knew I hadn't taken a nap here on purpose.

I'm not just any zombie: I'm a zombie *detective*, and it's my job to figure out mysteries. I'm good at my job—though I try to avoid being part of the mystery itself.

The coffin was dark and cramped, with very little elbow room. I squirmed, thumped the sides of the box with my arms, managed to roll myself over onto my stomach—which did me no good at all—then had to exert twice as much effort to roll myself onto my back again.

I pounded the wooden lid with my fists. Yes, it's a cliché: I had become one of those things that go bump in the night.

I felt the entire coffin vibrating beneath me, accompanied by a low pleasant thrumming. No wonder I had dozed off for so long! But this wasn't a timed "Magic Massage Fingers" sensation. I realized the sound was road noise, the vibration of wheels.

I was in the back of a vehicle somewhere.

Worse, I was in a coffin in the back of a vehicle going somewhere.

I hammered on the lid of the coffin, felt around the edge. No safety latch there. That was a code violation, and I was starting to feel testy.

Coffins are supposed to have quick-release latches, otherwise it's a safety hazard. Ever since the Big Uneasy, laws had changed to protect the unnaturals. My partner Robin had hung out her attorney-for-hire shingle on behalf of the vampires, zombies, werewolves, ghosts, and other assorted "beings" that needed legal representation in the changing world. One of her early legal victories was to institute safety systems in coffins and crypts so that, in the event that a dead body came back to life, he or she could re-emerge without discomfort or inconvenience.

I got my hands in front of my chest, flattened my palms, and pushed up against the coffin lid. The planks creaked but remained fastened. Nailed shut. This was getting more annoying by the minute.

I tried to remember where I'd been and how I'd gotten there, but it was all a big blank. I'm better-preserved than most zombies, many of whom eat brains because they have a deficiency in that department (kind of like a vitamin deficiency). Me, I've always loved a good cheeseburger, but these days I rarely bother to eat except out of habit, or sociability. I don't have much appetite, and my taste buds aren't what they used to be.

My mind, though, is sharp as a tack ... usually. Otherwise, I wouldn't be much of a detective. At present, I felt as blank and stupid as one of those shamblers who can only remember long strings of vowels without any consonants.

Moving in the cramped box now, I patted myself down and realized that I still wore my usual sport jacket with the lumpy threads where the bullet holes had been crudely stitched up. I managed to get my fingers up to my face, felt the cold skin, ran them up around my forehead and skull, felt a crater there—a bullet hole, entry wound in the back of my head, exit wound in my forehead.

Yes, everything seemed normal.

For many years, I'd been a detective in the Unnatural Quarter, a human detective at first, working on cases where unnaturals ran afoul of the law, or stumbled into curses, or just lost things from their original lives. I made a decent living at it, especially after I partnered with Robin, and the cases we dealt with were more interesting than typical adultery spying for divorce cases.

On the downside, I had ended up getting shot in the back of the head while investigating the poisoning death of my girlfriend. That would have been the end of any regular Sam Spade or Philip Marlowe, but the cases don't solve themselves, so when I came back from the dead … I went right back to work.

I pressed hard against the lid of the coffin again, heard the boards creak, listened to the nails groan a little bit. That was some progress, at least. I kept pushing.

Even though zombies have the advantage of being able to sleep wherever they like, vampires are generally more limber. I was accustomed to stiff muscles and sore joints, however, so I kept pushing. I put my back into it. (What, was I going to get a bruise?) With steady pressure, I managed to coax the nails farther out. The boards splintered, and the lid finally came loose.

I nudged the top of the coffin aside by a few inches and let in some cool air. But I was still trapped.

A thick silver chain and a padlock had been wrapped around the coffin. Great. Silver chains and a nailed-down coffin—exactly what would be required to contain a vampire. Okay, B+ for effort, but somebody really needed to go back to the field guides and do a better job at identifying their unnaturals.

How could anyone have confused me for a vampire?

Then one or two of the pieces fell into place with a big thud. I wasn't supposed to be here—this should have been someone else! I'd been duped, or switched.

Finally, I remembered about the witness protection program.

At Chambeaux & Deyer investigations, we take all sorts of cases—from a monster in trouble who lumbers through our doors, to humans having trouble with monsters, to monsters having trouble with one another. There's never a dull moment.

Occasionally, we get cases punted to us from the police, usually because Officer Toby McGoohan, my best human friend, brings them to us. McGoo appreciated the extra help on his backlog, and we appreciated the business.

McGoo and I were old friends well before I got shot—a down-on-his-luck private detective and a politically incorrect, often rude, beat cop with no prospects for promotion, even in the Unnatural Quarter. Some friendships survive even death. If I could put up with McGoo's lousy jokes, he could put up with my cadaverous infirmities.

He showed up in our offices wearing his full patrolman uniform and blue cap, leading a man in a ridiculous disguise: a trenchcoat, a wide-brimmed hat, and a curly wig that Harpo Marx would have found too extreme.

"Hey, Shamble," McGoo said. I had long since stopped objecting to his nickname for me, a deliberate mispronunciation of my last name.

When he didn't introduce his companion, I nodded to the stranger. "Correct me if I'm wrong, McGoo, but a disguise isn't supposed to *draw* attention."

The man in the goofy wig muttered, "I didn't want anyone to recognize me." He looked around, then muttered to McGoo, "Are we safe here?"

"Safe enough. These people are going to help get you into the witness protection program."

The man took off the hat, silly wig, and trenchcoat, to reveal he was a slight-framed blond man, as scrawny and skittish as if he had stepped right off the "before" side of a muscle supplement ad. He was a vampire.

"Let me introduce Sebastian Bund," McGoo said, "former blood barista at one of the Talbot & Knowles blood bars. He's also a key witness in an important case involving the illicit blood market."

Scrawny Sebastian slicked back his blond hair, which had been mussed by the wig. "Thank you for your help … as soon as you help."

Our receptionist at Chambeaux & Deyer is my girlfriend—and former client—Sheyenne. She's a ghost now, and I had been investigating her murder when I got killed, but we're still a couple. Many spirits linger because they have unfinished business, but even after I solved Sheyenne's murder, she remained, and she works for us now. Apparently her "unfinished business" now involved typing and filing in our offices. Chambeaux & Deyer couldn't have functioned without her.

"Could I get you some coffee or tea, or blood, Mr. Bund?" she asked, as she dropped the intake paperwork on her desk.

"Do you have any B-positive?" Bund asked.

"I think we just keep O in stock for the clients."

Bund shook his head. "Never mind. I can't stand the generic stuff. I'm fine."

McGoo pushed the papers aside. "There can't be any record of this. Everything off-book."

Sheyenne frowned. "Then how do we send our bill?"

"I'll take care of it, don't worry. I'll find a way to get it out of petty cash."

"If it's only petty cash," she countered, "then maybe the case isn't worth our time."

"We have a big petty cash fund."

Robin came out to meet the new client as well, looking friendly now, but when she sinks her teeth into a case, she's as hard to shake as a zombie with lockjaw. We went into the conference room together, so McGoo could explain the case to us.

Sebastian Bund had been caught up in under-the-counter blood sales, watering down the product, selling the extra out a back alley and using a seemingly legitimate blood bank to move his supplies. He would swap out rare and expensive types for more generic flavors. No one had noticed … until one of the mislabeled packets was actually used in surgery rather than for unnatural consumption, and the patient nearly died.

The plot unraveled, arrests were made, and the operation was pinned on an ambitious gangster family led by Ma Hemoglobin. (Her real last name was Hamanubin, but nobody referred to her by that.)

She had six sons, two of whom were vampires. Ma Hemoglobin and her boys ran blood-smuggling operations throughout the Quarter.

The District Attorney had vowed to bring them down. The owners of the Talbot & Knowles blood-bar chain (former clients of mine, I'm pleased to say) were eager to press charges.

"Unfortunately, each witness who would have testified against Ma Hemoglobin suffered an unfortunate demise," McGoo said.

"Is there such thing as a fortunate demise?" I asked. McGoo ignored the interruption; I think he was annoyed that he hadn't thought of the joke himself.

Several vampire witnesses had "accidentally" been locked in sunlit cells, and their ashes weren't in any shape to testify. Some of the human witnesses were assigned to vampires-only holding cells, and after the prisoner meals were "accidentally delayed" by several hours, the human witnesses were too drained to be of any use and "accidentally" contaminated with holy water during the resuscitation efforts so they couldn't even be turned into vamps themselves (thus, doubly prevented from taking the stand against Ma Hemoglobin). Another particularly important witness had vanished from a locked bathroom, and the only evidence was a brownish-green slime all around the toilet. There were rumors of sewer-dweller hit men who came up through the porcelain access to strike their target.

"Sebastian is the only witness left," McGoo said. "And obviously our traditional police protection methods haven't worked."

"Sounds like you need a zombie detective," I said.

"We need someone competent. Sebastian has to go into witness protection until the case comes up for trial."

Robin just nibbled on her pencil, deep in thought. "So you need our help to make sure he's moved without being seen."

McGoo nodded. "We've already got an operation under contract. He'll be taken cross-country in a coffin in the back of an eighteen-wheeler. We'll disguise the truck, make it look like it's hauling pre-packaged school lunches."

I cringed, and Robin shuddered, both of us remembering our own experiences with school lunches. "No one's going to mess with that cargo."

So, McGoo already had the general plan and his connections to the police force. We just had to work out the details.

Obviously, as the ominous voice always says in movie trailers, *something went wrong.* I wasn't the one who was supposed to be riding in the coffin. Somebody had set me up.

Once I pushed the loosened coffin lid to one side, I began to work on the silver chains and padlock. Fortunately, silver has no effect on me—that's an advantage to being a zombie, and I try to look at the glass as half full.

As a detective, I'm quite proficient, or at least marginally adequate, with lockpick tools that I keep in a handy travel pack in my pants pocket. My fingers were clumsy, but no more than usual. I worked with the tools until I sprung the padlock, removed the hasp, and shoved the chains to the floor.

Just as I sat up, the semi truck hit a bump in the road, which made the coffin thump against the trailer bed. My teeth clacked together, and then the hum of the road became smooth again. I knocked the lid to the floor and lurched up out of the coffin.

This was actually easier than when I had clawed my way up through the packed graveyard soil back when I first rose from the dead—not to mention a lot less dirty, too.

The truck rumbled along, and I stepped out of the coffin, flexing my stiff knees, stretching, brushing the wrinkles in my sport jacket. I looked around the coffin, but saw no sign of my fedora. I hoped it wasn't lost.

Even though my leaky brain had recaptured the basic story of Sebastian Bund going into witness protection, there were still many gaps. Once again, I felt around my head, but discovered no lumps. It's difficult to knock a zombie unconscious by bonking him on the head, anyway. There must have been something else, maybe a sleeping potion. I felt groggy, rubbed my eyes, still trying to get awake.

"Coffin" and "coffee" both derive from the root word "caffeine," I think—and I could have used a strong cup right now to help wake the dead. I needed to be alert, to judge whether I might be in danger.

Inside the trailer, other crates were stacked high all around where the coffin had been stashed. The crates were all filled with prepackaged school lunches; from the "Use By" dates stamped on the sides, they would not expire for more than a century.

I worked my way toward the front of the trailer, hoping I could find some way to signal the cab. The driver up there needed to know he had the wrong cargo. If someone had knocked me out and switched me with Sebastian Bund, then the star witness might be in danger.

The engine noise was loud, but I leaned against the wall and started pounding as hard as I could. (For a trucker hauling coffins filled with the undead, that would probably be unnerving.) If he had the window open, maybe he'd be able to hear me back here. I pounded harder and then, to reassure him, hammered out "Shave and a Haircut."

Faintly, from the cab, I heard him pound back on the door, "Two Bits."

I pounded harder, more desperately. He pounded back, and I heard his muffled voice. "Quiet back there!"

So much for raising the alarm. I guess I would have to wait until he stopped for a potty break—I hoped he had a small bladder.

I sat back down on the edge of the coffin, slipped my hands into the jacket pockets—and felt immediately stupid when I found my phone. That would have been a good thing to remember from the start. I didn't like all these lapses in my memory. Could a zombie get a concussion?

Since I had no idea where the truck was, possibly out in the middle of nowhere, I hoped that I'd get a signal. I was pleased to see at least one-and-a-half bars; that should be good enough.

I kept McGoo's number on speed-dial, and he picked up on the second ring. He must have seen the Caller ID. "Shamble! What are you doing awake already?"

"Trying to figure out where the hell I am." He didn't sound surprised to hear from me. "You sound like you know more about this than I do."

McGoo snorted. "I know more about most things than you do."

"I'd argue with that, but today I'll give you a free pass if you can tell me why I woke up in a nailed-shut coffin surrounded by silver chains in the back of a semi truck."

"Silver chains? There weren't supposed to be any silver chains."

I stared at the phone, then put it back to my ear.

"*That's* the part you find unusual? Why am I here in the first place?"

"It was your idea, Shamble, but if you don't remember your own brilliant solution, I'll take credit for it. The narcomancer said you might suffer some temporary memory loss as a side effect. It was a powerful spell."

"Narcomancer?" The word meant nothing to me, and I couldn't call any image to mind. "Don't you mean 'necromancer'?"

"*Narco*—narcomancer," McGoo said. "I suppose you've forgotten you owe me a hundred bucks, too?"

"I don't owe you a hundred bucks. But narcomancer … like in narcotics?"

"No, like narcolepsy. His name was Rufus. He's a wizard who worked a spell to put you to sleep—and putting a zombie to sleep is no easy task."

"Rufus?" The name still didn't ring a bell.

And suddenly, it did.

I recalled the man whose matted mouse-brown hair seemed to have a moral disagreement with combs. His wispy beard looked as if someone had been experimenting with spirit gum and theatrical makeup but had given up halfway through the job. His watery blue eyes were extremely bloodshot, and he seemed jittery. Although he specialized in putting people to sleep, he seemed to be an insomniac himself.

I remember him rubbing his hands together, repeating his name and grinning. "Yes, Rufus … are you ready for my special *roofie*? You'll snooze away the journey."

He began to speak an incantation—then everything went blank.

"It's all going down as planned," McGoo said on the phone. "We made all the arrangements for Sebastian to be whisked away in the truck to his new home, but we put you in the coffin instead, under a sleep spell—it was *supposed* to last for the entire drive—while Sebastian went by a roundabout route. A brilliant idea, actually. I suggested it."

"No, you didn't," I said. "That was my idea."

"I thought you didn't remember."

"But why would we *do* that?"

McGoo said, "Just to be safe. You were triggered to wake up if anyone tampered with the coffin. You were worried something bad might go down."

At that moment, an explosion hit the truck, blowing out the side of the trailer, scattering packaged school lunches everywhere, and hurling me out into the pitch-black night.

2

The squeal of the truck's air brakes would have made a banshee envious. The semi jack-knifed, its wheels smearing rubber along the highway like black fingerpaint. The truck groaned to a halt with a cough and gasp, and debris rained down everywhere.

After being thrown from the truck, I landed in a ditch—a mud-filled ditch, of course. I got to my feet, dripping; stagnant slime oozed out of my hair. It seems the harder I work to keep myself well-preserved, the faster karma comes back and smacks me.

The door to the truck cab popped open, and a stocky man with a black jawline beard swung out. His eyes burned like coals, and even from a distance I could tell he was hopping mad. He wore a trucker's cap, a red checked flannel shirt open to show his white undershirt, and jeans. He didn't seem injured, just furious as he stepped away from the wheezing and gurgling diesel engine that fought to keep running.

He stared at the ruined trailer, where a blackened crater and splintered wood surrounded the remnants of a slogan: "The Finest in Processed Lunches—Tolerated by Children for over Twenty Years!" On the image, a group of gaunt boys and girls looked dubiously toward the picture of their meal, which had been obliterated by the blast.

"They blew up my rig!" The trucker stalked back and forth, twisted his cap around backward, then, dissatisfied, twisted it back around front. "Out here on an empty stretch of highway? *They blew up my rig!*" He kicked gravel with his steel-toed boots, then looked up and saw me shambling toward him. "Did you see that?" Then he glowered, giving me a second look. "Where did you come from?"

"I was inside your truck," I said. "I'm Dan Chambeaux, private investigator."

The trucker blinked, still suspicious. "And I'm Earl—Earl Joe Bob, owner and operator of Earl Joe Bob Trucking." He scratched his beard. "Say, what were you doing in that coffin? You weren't supposed to be in there."

"Ever hear those stories about babies being switched in the nursery?"

"Yeah," he said.

"I guess it happens with coffins, too."

Earl Joe Bob put his hands on his hips and swung his head from side to side, looking in dismay at his mortally wounded rig. Under the bright running lights, which could have given a Christmas tree on the Las Vegas Strip a run for its money, I saw "Earl Joe Bob Trucking" and a phone number, as well as government license number on the driver's door. He sighed. "At least the cab and engine are still intact. But damn—I'm liable for all this! And, hey, you weren't supposed to be in that coffin!" He shook his head again, stuck his thumbs into the waistband of his jeans. "What a mess."

At least the trailer hadn't caught fire, though some of the shards of wood still smoldered. "I think we were hit with a rocket launcher."

"It happens," said Earl Joe Bob. He went back to the cab, got some flares and reflective hazard triangles.

I realized that out here on this open and silent stretch of highway, under the stars and with no city lights in sight, we were much too vulnerable. This truck hadn't run into a random migratory rocket. I patted my pockets, looked around—I had lost my phone during the explosion.

"We have to call for help. Can we use your CB? Or a cell phone?"

Earl Joe Bob shook his head. "No, wouldn't be wise to use it."

I was exasperated. "Why not?"

The trucker narrowed his eyes at me. "Just can't."

I couldn't argue with that logic. I walked around the other side of the truck again, working my way back to the ditch, where I hunted around for my phone. The weeds were tall, and I splashed through the standing water. Mosquitoes fled from me—another advantage of being a zombie. I would have to write all the advantages down one day, just as a reminder.

Fortunately, the phone's screen light was still on, though my call with McGoo had been disconnected in the explosion. I smeared it against my muddy shirt, making a marginally clean patch, and was dismayed to see that my Angry Vultures scores had been wiped out. That was a problem I would have to deal with later.

I phoned McGoo, who answered right away. "Where are you, Shamble? What happened?"

"I'm on a road somewhere," I said, glancing around. "And I don't see one of those You Are Here X's." I told McGoo about the explosion, and that we were stranded. He promised to call in reinforcements right away.

"I'll see if we can track your signal through the cell towers," he said. "Maybe the truck has a GPS in the cab."

I ended the call and began making my way along the back of the rig, when I froze, hearing voices. I saw two figures approach the wounded truck. It was a starlit night, clear skies, a quarter moon. Zombie night vision is generally good, but I didn't need any supernatural powers to pick out the two young men. They wore camouflage jumpsuits—but light-colored desert camo, so they stood out plainly. They carried long rifles.

Since the side of the truck had been blasted open with a rocket launcher, and since these two men were approaching heavily armed, I decided it wouldn't be a good idea to wave my arms and hail them for help.

Earl Joe Bob spotted them as well, and bunched his meaty arms as he stalked toward them. "This wasn't the deal I had with Ma Hemoglobin! Which two of her boys are you—Moron and Imbecile?"

"No," said one of the young men. "I'm Huey, and that's Louis."

"Well, you're still Moron and Imbecile to me. You wrecked my rig! We were supposed to meet up at the Rest In Peace area down the road and make the transfer!" He spluttered, waving his hand at the crater in the side of his truck. "What kind of stupid—"

The two boys raised their rifles. Huey said, "Ma thought you might double-cross us, so we took matters into our own hands."

"You must be two of her human boys," Earl Joe Bob said. "A vampire wouldn't be that stupid."

"We'll show you stupid!" said Louis. He opened fire with his high-powered rifle. Not to be left behind, Huey shot Earl Joe Bob as well. The bullets slammed into the trucker's red flannel shirt, and he dropped to the ground.

I silently reaffirmed my wisdom in not waving my arms and calling attention to myself.

Now, as a detective, I solve cases, and I'm the hero in my own story. But sometimes heroes stick around longer if they aren't always … heroic.

I didn't know how I was going to get out of here, or how long it would take McGoo to bring in reinforcements. If this truck was on a cross-country trip to deliver a decoy into witness protection, McGoo could be miles away, even if he had been shadowing me.

With a jolt, I got a few more of my memories back: I did remember the idea of taking Sebastian's place in the coffin aboard the truck. Meanwhile, Robin would take our nondescript and rusty old Ford Maverick, lovingly named the Pro Bono Mobile, with the scrawny blond vampire dressed in my fedora and a similar sport jacket, sunshades down, traveling across the state line to where he would be hidden in his new life. My ghost girlfriend Sheyenne was going to ride shotgun. Nobody would be looking for them. They would be safe. It would be a lark. I was the one under a narcolepsy spell in the back of a semi truck, a decoy. It should have been a long sleep for me.

Now, Ma Hemoglobin's two boys climbed through the blasted crater in the side of the trailer. My best bet was probably to climb back into the ditch and hide in the mud, but McGoo would never let me forget it.

Instead, I crept along the opposite side of the trailer. If I could make it to the cab, open the passenger side door, and climb into the cab, I was sure to find some kind of firearm, baseball bat, or tire iron that Earl Joe Bob kept there.

I heard Huey and Louis rummaging around inside the trailer, shining flashlights; I saw the gleam through splintered cracks in the opposite wall. They tossed aside a clutter of prepackaged school lunches. "The coffin's empty! He's not here!"

The other voice said, "I hate it when coffins turn up empty! But was it empty in the first place, or were we tricked?"

I made it to the front of the rig, yanked open the cab door—and of course the hinges screeched and groaned loudly enough to make any haunted house proud. The two Hemoglobin boys clambered out of the blasted trailer, brandishing their rifles, looking around.

"There he is!" yelled Louis.

"I see him," said Huey. They began sprinting toward me, running past the body of Earl Joe Bob, who lay sprawled at the side of the truck.

Earl groaned and sat up, shaking his head. "Dammit! You wrecked my rig *and* you shot me?" He sprang to his feet and flashed a set of ivory fangs.

I should have recognized earlier that he was a vampire. Many truckers who specialize in all-night hauls are vampires; they have no trouble staying awake, though they had to park in Rest In Peace areas and pull down the shades by dawn.

The two Hemoglobin boys turned white and spun around, raising their rifles again. Each managed to fire one more shot. This time, Earl Joe Bob merely flinched before lunging forward again.

"I thought you loaded the rifles with silver bullets!" Huey shouted.

"I thought *you* loaded the rifles with silver bullets!"

Earl Joe Bob was pissed.

Moving with vampire speed (earlier, I did mention that vamps can be quite swift and agile), he lunged forward and grabbed the young men by their necks, one in each hand. His grip was powerful, and he squeezed hard. I heard the loud double-crack as their necks snapped; it sounded like popcorn in a microwave bag. He tossed the two dead bodies on the ground—truly dead, because Huey and Louis had been two of Ma Hemoglobin's four human sons. (These days one or the other could still come back as an unnatural, but it wouldn't be anytime soon.)

Earl Joe Bob made a disgusted sound, brushed at his flannel shirt, looked down at the bullet holes healing in his chest. "I'm as much a mess as my rig is." He saw me hanging onto the door and flashed his fangs. "And where do you think you're going?"

The vampire trucker moved toward me. I held up my cell phone as if inviting him to play a game of Curses With Friends. "I already called in for help. The police are coming."

Earl Joe Bob scowled. "That doesn't give me much time, then. It wasn't supposed to go down this way." He straightened his cap, which sat askew from when he'd been gunned down. He sneered at the two Hemoglobin boys, who lay in their light camouflage on the ground, necks bent at improbable angles. "I hate dealing with amateurs. I've dealt with witness protection cases plenty of times, and I'm always available for additional 'enhanced disappearing' for a substantial fee. When I make people disappear, I really make them disappear."

I tried to move along the side of the truck; in a race, I could never outrun the vampire. "Isn't that a conflict of interest?"

"I don't lose any sleep over it," Earl Joe Bob said. "Pay is good, and I gotta earn a living."

I knew that he was going to have to get rid of me. I was the only one who could explain the mess around me, but Earl Joe Bob would make up some story of his own.

"We can be reasonable about this," I offered.

"Good idea." He lunged. I lurched—it was a much less fluid movement than his, but I did manage to evade the first pass. Earl Joe Bob slammed into the side of the trailer, shattering more wood.

"Careful about the splinters." My mind was racing. I could get one of the jagged spears and thrust it through the vampire's heart. In my imagination, it all worked out just fine, but in practice I wasn't quite the nimble athlete that I'd need to be for the scheme to work.

I did break off the long wooden splinter, lifted it—and Earl Joe Bob slapped it out of my hands. At least he got a splinter in his palm, and he paused to pluck it out. That brief respite gave me the chance to scramble through the blasted crater in the side of the trailer.

"Now I've got you cornered," the trucker said. While I shuffled and slipped among the debris of packaged school lunches, I saw his sturdy muscular form silhouetted against the starlit sky as he pulled himself through the hole. "Where are you going to hide?"

I hurled a package of Salisbury steak, which struck him in the center of the chest. Unfortunately, it wasn't quite the stake through the heart I required. The vamp trucker's eyes were glowing in the shadows. I could see him coming toward me. I nearly tripped backward over the coffin that had held me during my cross-country trip.

Police sirens howled down the highway, coming closer. Ironic, I thought: the cavalry was going to arrive much too late.

"At least we've already got a coffin to store you in," said Earl Joe Bob.

"Been there, done that," I answered.

He came closer, fangs bared, eyes glowing, hands outstretched. Earl Joe Bob was a burly guy, powerful enough to change one of his eighteen tires simply by lifting the rig and undoing the lug nuts with his fingertips. He could probably rip me limb from limb, stomp on any pieces still twitching, and then claim I'd been mangled in the explosion. McGoo already knew better than that.

"You haven't thought this through," I said.

The trucker laughed. "I could say the same to you—a vampire versus a zombie? The vamp will win, every time." He reached toward me.

That's when I pulled up the loose silver chains that lay draped over the coffin. I threw them onto Earl Joe Bob.

"Not every time," I said.

It was like Superman and Kryptonite—a real sight to see. Within seconds, the vamp trucker went from being a scary, overpowering opponent to a whimpering and helpless guy in a flannel shirt who squirmed under the chains.

"Awww crap!" Earl Joe whined. "That's not fair!"

Now the sirens were louder, and I could see the flashing lights through the hole in the side of the truck. Squad cars raced along the highway, followed by the state patrol. I was still undead and kicking, but I no longer needed them to rescue me. Still, I'd be happy to let McGoo handle the wrap-up paperwork.

As soon as the police climbed into the trailer, I waved McGoo over. He looked flushed and worried. "Shamble, you all right?"

There were shouts outside as other officers found the two bodies of Ma Hemoglobin's boys.

"Better than they are. And better than he is." I nodded to where Earl Joe Bob squirmed on the floor under the silver chains.

His cap had fallen off in the struggle, and I reached down and plucked it up. It wasn't my style—I much preferred the fedora, but that was gone for now, apparently on the head of a disguised Sebastian Bund. Since I felt naked without a hat, I settled the trucker cap in place.

I started rattling off the full story as an officer handcuffed Earl Joe Bob with silver-plated handcuffs. The vamp trucker spluttered and groaned at the way I described a few things, but he didn't deny any of the details.

"I'll cut a deal," he said. "Ma Hemoglobin is scary, and she's got four boys left. I'll turn State's witness. Put me into witness protection, otherwise I'll never survive until the trial." His eyes flashed, and he struggled against the silver handcuffs. "I know where all the bodies are buried—some of them more than once."

3

Back in the offices, Robin and Sheyenne were both in very good moods, having delivered Sebastian Bund to his official new undisclosed location.

"He was delightful company." Robin flashed a smile at me. "Did you know he used to be a singing barista?"

"Broadway show tunes," Sheyenne said. "That's all we talked about. He's a fan of musicals. Why don't you ever see musicals with me?"

"Because I don't like musicals," I said.

She gave me a spectral raspberry. "When you go out on a date, you're supposed to do something you don't like. That's how you show a girl you care for her."

"I'll keep that in mind next time we go out on a date." Our cases almost always interfered with our love life—and so did the fact that, as a ghost, she couldn't physically touch me, which made the intimate aspect of our relationship much more problematic. "Did we at least get paid for the case?"

"We got paid in satisfaction," Robin said. "That's our purpose here, to know that justice is done."

"Right." I turned to Sheyenne, repeating the question. "Did we at least get paid?"

She showed me a Chambeaux & Deyer invoice, on which she had merely written in capital letters: SERVICES RENDERED, no other details. "Officer McGoohan was true to his word." She pulled out a stack of other pending cases and floated ahead to place the files on my desk. "One more step in making the world safe for naturals and unnaturals everywhere."

"It's a start." I looked down at all the folders Sheyenne had gotten out, and I knew exactly what they were. Job security.

Naughty & Nice

1

Santa Claus was an *unnatural.* That made perfect sense—I just hadn't thought of it before.

The jolly bearded guy in the bright-red suit came into the offices of Chambeaux & Deyer Investigations, desperate to hire my services. It's not often, I suppose, that Santa requires a detective—particularly a zombie detective.

"I need your help, Mr. Chambeaux," Santa said.

I extended my gray hand to shake his black-gloved one. "At your service."

I assessed my client-to-be. Santa carried a voluminous cloth sack over his left shoulder; it was limp and empty at the moment, rather than bulging with brightly wrapped gifts. His bloodshot eyes were as red as his suit. His cheeks were pale, and his face seemed less plump than the pictures I had seen on a million Christmas cards.

"It's a crisis." He looked around with haunted eyes. "I've been robbed!"

In the Unnatural Quarter, we see all sorts of clients. After the Big Uneasy, all manner of legendary creatures had reappeared: ghosts, vampires, zombies, werewolves, ghouls, and other creatures that go bump, growl, or thud in the night. Why not Santa, too? Somebody who can slip down billions of chimneys in a night—without incurring a single home-invasion charge—would fit right in.

"We'll do everything we can to help, Mr. Claus," said Robin Deyer, as she came out to greet the new client. "Is this more of a legal matter or an investigative one?"

"Oh-ho-ho, I definitely need a detective, and I came here because Mrs. Claus and I have heard about Mr. Chambeaux."

I was surprised. "We don't even advertise up at the North Pole. How did you find out about Chambeaux and Deyer Investigations?"

"Actually, we're local. My powers only manifest during the holiday season—it's not a full-time gig up in the cold. The rest of the year Mrs. Claus and I run a nice little bed-and-breakfast in the Quarter. Everybody around town knows the zombie detective to call when they're in a bind."

When I first moved into the Unnatural Quarter, I was a regular human P.I., trying to make a living like anybody else. I catered to clients who, though they sometimes looked like monsters on the outside, still had very human problems. Even after I got myself killed on a case, I climbed out of the grave and got back to work, still with Robin as my partner. Most unnaturals aren't even bothered by the bullet hole in the middle of my forehead, and I've stopped being self-conscious about applying morticians' putty to cover it up.

Sheyenne flitted up to Santa, beaming her gorgeous smile. "May I take your coat, Mr. Claus?"

Not only is Sheyenne extremely smart, competent, and efficient, she's beautiful on all counts. She's also my girlfriend. On top of that, she happens to be a ghost, murdered in the same case that saw me dead. But even through all that, we stuck together. It's a testament to the strength of our relationship.

Santa decided against removing his red coat. "No-ho-ho! It's part of my traditional image. The coat is made of magical material that keeps me comfortable no matter the temperature. That way I never have to take it off until the season's over. Traditions are important, and never more so than around the holidays."

Sheyenne leaned closer and whispered, "For the record, I never stopped believing in you."

He regarded Sheyenne with both wonder and mirth. "Strangely enough, I didn't believe in ghosts—until a few years ago." Santa sneezed, then turned back to me. "Mr. Chambeaux, I'm not going to kid you. There's more riding on this particular Christmas than ever before, and I'm coming apart at the seams. I need you to find my stolen property before Christmas Eve, or there'll be no joy to the world, no ho-ho-ho, no holly jolly, no Feliz in the Navidad, no Frohe in the Weihnachten, no Merry in the Christmas. You see how serious this is?"

"I think I do." I really had no idea, but I didn't want to look dumb in front of Santa Claus. "What exactly was stolen?"

"My list!" He was distraught—which was not at all the sort of attitude I expected from a man famous for his rumbling belly laugh and infectious good cheer. "My *list* of who's Naughty and Nice! Without that list, I won't know which houses to visit, which Johnny deserves a model train set and which one gets a lump of coal, which Susie deserves a doll and which one gets a boring sweater. If I can't figure that out, Christmas definitely won't be the most wonderful time of the year."

"Don't you keep a photocopy?" Robin asked. "Or an on-line backup?"

Santa was horrified. "And break Christmas tradition? Millions of children believe in me and the way I do things, just so. They have dreams about Christmas, and it's my responsibility to safeguard those dreams." He shook his head again. "If I modernized, there'd be an uproar—not to mention countless bugs in the system—and then you can bet the Easter Bunny would hack into my database and start grabbing my market share. No, everything's done by hand on a very long roll of parchment, the names of every single boy and girl written with a goose quill."

That must have been the world's largest two-column spreadsheet. "And how exactly was it stolen?"

"Someone broke into the offices of my North Pole headquarters. It's our busy season, all of my helpers doing double shifts, decking the halls, dashing through the snow. Our packaging department is a madhouse, full of complete sets of lords a-leaping, partridges, pear trees—and everybody wants five golden rings. We still have an overstock of last year's fruitcakes, and I don't know what to do with the figgy puddings. I was sure there'd be a demand for those again." He wiped a gloved hand across his forehead.

"It's very hectic. I was taking a break with Mrs. Claus. She had made a fresh batch of eggnog, and this time of year she spikes it rather heavily. I slept like a baby … and when I went back to the office the list was gone!" He tugged on his beard. "It had to be an inside job." He paced back and forth, scuffing his black boots on our all-weather carpet. "I checked with all the line supervisor elves and every single one of the toy builders. This time of year they work around the clock without even restroom or cigarette breaks. But everyone had an alibi."

"Could you have been targeted by Homeland Security?" Robin asked. "Or some other law-enforcement organization monitoring your research as to who might be on a Most Naughty list?"

"I can see why they might want that," I said.

"Not at all, I have a close cooperative relationship with government agencies, considering all that airspace I fly over—and my work has to be done in a single night, so I have no time to mess with clearances. I even let NORAD track me every year. No, that list is in the hands of someone who means no good, mark my words … and no human could have gotten through my security. It had to be an unnatural."

He hung his head and seemed so sad that I wanted to sit on Santa's lap and give him a hug. He continued, "That's why I came to you, Mr. Chambeaux. If I don't get that Naughty and Nice list in time, I can't stop thinking about all those poor children who'll be disappointed, all those broken dreams, all those undelivered presents. It'll destroy their faith in Christmas … and they just might turn out to be naughty next year."

I was determined to solve the problem. It's not every day you get a chance to save Christmas—and not just because Christmas only comes once a year. "Don't underestimate how relentless a zombie can be, Santa. I'll find your list. If I have any questions or developments, how will I get hold of you? Do you have a business card?"

"Much better than that." Santa reached into a pocket of his red jacket and pulled out a bright green ribbon with a jingle bell attached. "Just ring this, and I'll be there. Even if I'm otherwise occupied, I have an answering service that can get hold of me."

The pink had come back to his cheeks, and a droll smile lifted his lips. "Oh-ho-ho, if you solve this case, there'll be something very special under the tree—for all of you."

Relieved and encouraged, Santa slung his empty sack over one shoulder and prepared to go. He closed his eyes and touched a finger to the side of his nose.

When nothing happened, he looked around our offices. Finding no chimney, he chuckled. "Sorry, I've been so worried about Christmas being ruined, I forgot how I arrived!" He left through the front door instead.

2

Although I knew I might have to go to Santa's North Pole seasonal offices to see the crime scene, I decided to search in the Unnatural Quarter first, which was much more convenient. (Riding up to the Arctic for hours in a freezing open sleigh sounded worse than flying in a middle seat in Coach.)

I started with someone who kept a similar list—primarily a Naughty list.

Officer Toby McGoohan is a dedicated beat cop, but his penchant for telling off-color jokes to the wrong people had gotten him transferred to the Quarter. McGoo is also my BHF, my best human friend. We help each other on cases. We commiserate about life and unlife over beers at the Goblin Tavern.

I found him outside one of the Talbot & Knowles blood bars, which are frequented by vampires who need their daily caffeine and hemoglobin fix. Some fanged customers drink straight blood, while others go for berry-flavored blood frappés or, now that the weather had turned colder, steaming cinnamon-spice hot clotties.

"Hey, Shamble," McGoo said, tipping his blue cap. "What do you get when you cross a snowman with a vampire?"

"What?" I groaned in advance.

"Frostbite." He persists in telling me jokes. I haven't been able to convince him they're not funny, and he hasn't been able to convince me that they are. As a special favor, I did promise I would try to laugh at some of them. But only some. "What's new and exciting in your world?"

"I just picked up Santa Claus as a client. Somebody stole his list of Naughty and Nice kids."

McGoo's eyes widened. "Well, that's a miracle on …" he glanced up, looking for a street corner, "32nd Street. If even Santa isn't safe from criminal activity, we are living in troubled times indeed. What does the list look like?"

"Long roll of parchment, millions of handwritten names. Two columns labeled N and N."

McGoo shook his head. "I'll keep an eye out, but we've got real problems of our own in the Quarter." He lowered his voice. "Kids are going missing, Shamble—a lot of them. We've received a rash of reports."

A vampire couple came out of the blood bar, chatting away. One held a to-go carrier with four cups of blood drinks marked with Type A (extra hot), Type O negative, and two with Type B positive (and a hand-drawn smiley face).

McGoo called, "Excuse me, can I see those for a second?"

The vampires turned, surprised. "What is it, Officer?"

"Your blood drinks. I want to show my friend something."

McGoo indicated the to-go cups, the first of which showed the printed picture of a young vampire boy who had been turned when he was maybe twelve years old. Big letters said "Have You Seen Me?" Printed below the photo were the vampire kid's name, pre-turned age, and last-seen data.

The second cup showed a zombie boy with an incongruous smile beneath his sunken eyes. The third was a scruffy-looking full-furred werewolf, and the fourth showed a human girl in Goth makeup wearing an off-the-shelf gloomy expression.

After he thanked the vampire couple, they left. I shook my head. "That's troubling, McGoo. I think I recognize the werewolf kid. He was part of the gang at the rumble a few months ago, Hairballs versus the Monthlies.

"Yeah, he's not the only rough one. Some of the missing children are straight off the Wikipedia page for Juvenile Delinquent. Not all of those photos were in a family album—a few are from mug-shot files."

"Some of the disappearances could just be runaways," I suggested. "Visiting some nice old lady's gingerbread house in the forest."

"For the record, Shamble, she wasn't a nice old lady—I worked on that case," McGoo said. "Not all of the missing kids have records.

We've got grieving parents or foster-parents who want to find their missing little angels. I don't know if the cases are related, or just a coincidence."

"I don't believe in coincidence," I said, wondering if this might also have something to do with the stolen Naughty and Nice list. "But I didn't believe in Santa Claus either, and now he's my client. Let me know if you get a lead on my case. I'll do the same if I hear anything about the missing kids."

McGoo nodded. "The Quarter's getting nervous—put your mind to it, see what you come up with. You've got a lot of space in that big empty head of yours."

I tapped the bullet hole in the middle of my forehead. "A little extra space maybe, but it's not empty." I tipped my fedora at him and left.

My first order of business was to figurc out who would *want* to steal the Naughty and Nice list, and what anybody would use it for. In order to brainstorm, I invited Sheyenne to lunch.

3

Being a ghost, Sheyenne doesn't eat, not even their special "ephemeral" plate, and I don't need much sustenance. (I've avoided brains, because I don't want to turn into one of *those* zombies who are an embarrassment to the rest of us.)

The Ghoul's Diner, though, was a place to hang out, and Sheyenne likes it when we go out on lunch dates. Strolling down the sidewalk toward the Diner, we free-associated. Sheyenne wore a bright smile as always, and those blue eyes could make a man's heart stop beating, or start beating, depending on which condition he started from.

I wondered aloud that maybe the Big Uneasy had made the Grinch manifest as well, but Sheyenne doubted he'd reached a worldwide cultural status similar to vampires or St. Nick. I disagreed, because I had grown up on the Grinch; still, I conceded that he seemed too obvious a cartoon villain.

I then postulated that the perpetrator could be a Lorax with self-esteem issues, upset that Arbor Day didn't have the stature of

Christmas, Hanukkah, Thanksgiving, New Years … or even Kwanzaa, for that matter. I didn't know if Loraxes were real, either. I seemed to be in a Seussian rut.

A light dusting of snow came down, reminding me that I had to find Santa's list before Christmas Eve, or he would suffer a worldwide toy-distribution crisis. Festive decorations were already strung up in the streets of the Quarter: barbed-wire tinsel looped along windowpanes and awnings, colorful wreaths hung from nooses on gallows lampposts.

Before we reached the Diner, Sheyenne and I stopped on the street where crowds had gathered and traffic halted for an early holiday parade. And it sure wasn't the type hosted by Macy's.

Elves capered and danced at the front of the parade, diminutive creatures dressed in pointed floppy caps and bright red outfits trimmed with white flocking. The costumes resembled a traditional Santa's elf suit, but these were cheap knockoffs that fit poorly with seams showing and with some of the white trim missing.

These elves were not the cute, smiling, industrious workers who stocked Santa's shelves and made the North Pole a cheery, if formerly imaginary, place. No, these elves came from the G-side of the family, having more in common with gremlins, goblins, and gnomes—pointy, stretched-out features, gray skin, and long ears that looked as if they had gotten caught in industrial picking machinery. When they smiled like good elves should, they showed alarmingly pointed teeth.

Behind the prancing elves came a bizarre motorized sleigh crawling along at pedestrian speed so everyone on the sidewalk had an appropriate opportunity to wave. Palm trees adorned the back of the sleigh. On a big wicker chair sat an elf with all the usual elf features (from the G-side of the family), but he wore a white rhinestone-studded jacket, trimmed in Christmasy green and red. He had slicked-back black hair, sideburns that extended halfway down his pointed chin, big garish sunglasses, and oddly out-of-place blue suede shoes.

"You've got to be kidding me," I said to Sheyenne.

"He's for real, Beaux. That's Elfis—I've seen his ads. You know, 'Santa Claus is coming to town, but Elfis will get there faster?' He's a celebrity on the cable-access channels."

I'm a decent enough detective, but I can be clueless about pop culture.

Elfis waved at the crowd and picked up a handheld Vegas-style silver microphone. "Thank ya very much. Santa's got competition this year, boys and girls, naturals and unnatural. The holidays should be for everybody, not just kids who pass some arbitrary naughty-or-nice test. Even naughty kids deserve presents, don't they?"

From the sidewalk crowds, a smattering of natural and unnatural children cheered—kids who knew they were included in the Naughty column, no doubt.

"Santa Claus has had a monopoly on the Christmas season for far too long—but I intend to undercut his position. Elfis Industries has wider distribution, more fairness, and less discrimination. More transparency in holiday gift-giving! We're going to expose all those 'secret admirer' gifts for what they are. And no more bribery with milk and cookies. *Everyone* deserves a present, and I'm the one to give it to them. It's time to put the kitsch back into Christmas!"

His elves began handing out candy canes, traditional red-and-white striped ones, blood-red ones, and black ones. A witch dressed in a midnight-blue gown and pointy cap stood by her young son who looked as if he might grow up to be a powerful necromancer. The boy ran forward to take a black candy cane, but his mother scolded him. "I told you not to take candy from strangers!"

The boy pouted. "He's not a stranger, Mom—that's *Elfis!*"

"Oh," the witch said, and handed him back the cane.

The motorized sleigh rolled by, with Elfis in his sequins and sunglasses waving from under his palm trees. He called out, "Who needs the cold? I have nightmares about a white Christmas! Let it snow, let it snow, let it snow—but somewhere far away! Stick with me, and the holidays will have a warm and sunny glow."

After the parade passed, Sheyenne leaned close to me. "So that's why Santa is so worried. He's got competition this year. And if his rival does a better job satisfying the customers …"

"Then Santa Claus won't be coming to town anymore," I said. "We might have our first suspect. Elfis has a motive to sabotage Santa's work. I better go talk to him and find out if his intentions really are as pure as new fallen snow."

I could tell this case was going to spell T-R-O-U-B-L-E.

4

After Sheyenne and I had a quick lunch at the diner (pink slime was on special), I went off to continue my investigation.

The headquarters for the competitive holiday operation was an office building in front of a fenced compound of airplane-hangar-sized structures, no doubt where Elfis manufactured and stored all the toys he planned to distribute ahead of his business rival. According to Sheyenne, Elfis's ads promised delivery by Christmas Eve Eve.

The sign at the front entrance had giant letters painted like candy canes, surrounded by yellow suns: "North Pole South: We're Better Because We're Closer to the Equator." Around the doorway was strewn blue sand or fake snow, which seemed incongruous … until I remembered "Blue Christmas."

When I entered the front door of North Pole South, I heard many busy bodies working in the back, but the reception counter was empty except for a fist-sized fake rock sitting on top of an index card that said "Ring bell for service." I picked up the stone and realized it was hollow. When I shook it, a tinkling chime rang out.

A female elf receptionist scurried out of the back, smiling sweetly with her pinched face. "I see you found our Jingle-Bell Rock," she snickered. "Very clever, don't you think? Elfis came up with it himself." She shuffled papers and handed me a temporary-employment application. "Looking for part-time holiday work? Many positions available."

I shook snow from the brim of my fedora. "That would be a conflict of interest. I've been retained by Santa Claus."

The receptionist's eyebrows rose. "I'll let Elfis know you're here." She took back the Jingle-Bell Rock and punched an extension on her phone. "He told us to expect an overture from Mr. Claus."

"Overture?" I asked. "I can barely hum a tune."

Elfis agreed to see me, probably out of curiosity; at least it got me through the door.

The chief elf's back office was bright and stiflingly hot. A large tropical mural covered the far wall. Wearing only a towel around his waist, Elfis lay back on a chaise lounge under a pair of heat lamps that could have been used to keep food warm in a restaurant.

Standing on either side, a pair of Egyptian mummies gently fanned him with palm fronds.

Elfis lifted his sunglasses and sat up to regard me. "Dan Chambeaux, Private Investigator … that seems an odd choice for Santa, but I knew he'd send a representative before long. He has no option but to open negotiations. I suppose he wants to suggest some kind of merger and keep a token title for himself? Frankly I'd rather just buy his operations outright."

He waved for the mummies to back away. "Would you like some refreshment? I can get one of my boys to make you a mai tai or piña colada. Or, if you want to be more traditional, I have chestnuts roasting on an open fire."

Chestnuts weren't the only things roasting. "I'm surprised you keep it so hot in here," I said, tugging at my collar—and zombies don't perspire.

Elfis explained, "I want to change the paradigm of the holiday season. It's too cold, too snowy, too wintry. You really think shepherds prefer to watch their flocks in the snow? They'd rather be skiing. And if I want something frozen, I order a frozen margarita." He laughed, but it sounded more like heh-heh-heh than ho-ho-ho.

"Now then, let's talk about sending old Saint Nick into retirement. Here's my offer: I take over all his operations, but I let him keep his North Pole annex. He and Mrs. Claus get a nice pension, run their bed-and-breakfast, maybe do a few public appearances for old times' sake, but I license his likeness and the brand. I'm dreaming of a profitable Christmas."

"There's been a misunderstanding, Mr. Elfis. That's not why I'm here."

The elf slicked back his hair, adjusted his position on the chaise lounge. The mummies came forward again to fan him vigorously with the palm fronds. "Well, then, I'm all ears."

"Santa Claus hired me as a detective because something very valuable was stolen from him."

Elfis seemed completely uninterested. "Really? And what would old St. Nick find valuable? Can't he just wiggle his nose and make another of whatever it was?"

"It's more of a matter of administrative records gone missing," I said. "I'm investigating the theft."

Elfis snickered. "You must mean his list. Anal-retentive, if you ask me." He slid his sunglasses back down on his face, scratched his sideburns. "And you think I had something to do with it? Why in the world would I need a list like that? I explicitly *don't* discriminate. I give presents to all kids, without scoring them on social behavior. What gives Santa the right to make a subjective decision about who's Naughty and Nice? Judgmental jerk, if you ask me." He sniffed. "I plan to take discrimination out of Christmas gift-giving, make it equal for all. What would be my motive for stealing the list?"

I did have a theory. "You'd hamstring Santa's activities, make him look incompetent, while gaining brownie points for yourself."

"I don't have brownies, Mr. Chambeaux. I have elves. There's a difference."

"That doesn't address my theory."

"Look around you, Mr. Chambeaux. I'm sabotaging Santa's work by perfectly traditional means—undercutting prices, faster distribution, more transparency in my operations. I don't need a list for that."

One of the mummies served him a cool drink in a hollowed pineapple, complete with a colorful umbrella. "Thank ya very much." Elfis took a long refreshing sip. "Tell Santa if he wants to come to terms, I'm having a holiday special. His decision. Either way, it's time he faced some competition."

Elfis reached down beside his chaise lounge and pulled out a baseball-sized knot of thorny leaves, like a wadded tumbleweed studded with berries. "Here, Mr. Chambeaux—have a free sample. Part of my effort to put the kitsch back into Christmas."

He tossed it to me, and I caught it. "What's this?"

"Our new McMistletoe. Cheaper to manufacture, no preservatives needed, non-poisonous, non-habit-forming." He spoke at such a fast pace that my ears could barely keep up. "It's not intended to diagnose, prevent, treat, or cure any disease. These claims have not been evaluated by the FDA." He grinned. "But our McMistletoe is just as effective as real mistletoe. Try it out, you'll see."

I pocketed the mistletoe in my jacket's other pocket, because it didn't seem right to tuck it beside the jingle bell that Santa Claus had given me. "I'll try it," I said, though I doubted Sheyenne would be impressed.

5

I was already disturbed about the missing children McGoo was investigating, but I didn't see the actual pain until the Tannenbaums came into our offices.

Mrs. Tannenbaum buried her face in her husband's broad chest. "Our baby boy!"

Both of them were werewolves—the Monthly variety, so they passed for normal except on full-moon nights. They seemed like a nice couple with modest lives, middle-income jobs, probably had a home that was not extravagant but one they were proud of.

Robin hurried forward to comfort them. "Tell us what happened."

Mr. Tannenbaum pulled a wallet from his pocket and showed us a snapshot. "This is our son Buddy." The kid was of the full-furred persuasion, the type of werewolf who maintained a long muzzle, sharp fangs, moist black nose, and facial fur throughout the month.

"That's his school portrait," Mrs. Tannenbaum said with a sniff. "He was just about to graduate sixth grade." Sheyenne flitted in with a tissue for the grieving woman.

I studied the snapshot. Buddy Tannenbaum's black lips were curled in what I assumed was a smile, but might have been a snarl. What kid didn't make a goofy face when sitting for a school portrait? "Not much family resemblance. Adopted?"

Mrs. Tannenbaum snuffled loudly. "He came from an abused home, and we took him in. Poor Buddy! We wanted to show him all the love and affection he deserved. But one day after school, he didn't come home to do his chores."

Her husband continued, "He often gets preoccupied with friends—he has a strong social life. And what's a chore or two around the house? No need to bother the boy with them. I can do the vacuuming and take out the garbage while my wife cooks dinner."

"On the night he disappeared, I made a fleshloaf with tomato sauce and onions. Buddy's favorite!" Mrs. Tannenbaum wailed, which came out as a trailing howl. "We had to eat it ourselves. We had leftovers for two days."

"Two days? Your son vanished and you didn't report it for two days?" Robin shot me a look, and I saw that furrow of concern on her brow.

"We thought he might be staying at a friend's house," said Mr. Tannenbaum. "He sometimes does that. We try not to be overprotective. A boy needs his space and … a wolf has to run free."

"Can you find him?" Mrs. Tannenbaum said. "We didn't want to go to the police because … because we want to keep his record clean. He's going to go to college someday, and it's really a private matter."

"You can count on our discretion, Mr. and Mrs. Tannenbaum." I doubted Buddy's disappearance was unrelated to the other children who had vanished.

"Can you give us the names of his friends, or places where he liked to spend time?" Robin asked.

Mrs. Tannenbaum considered. "He likes to hang out at the comic-book shop. Just Dug Up Collectibles, I think it's called."

"I know the place," I said. "I've been there."

In a fit of nostalgia, I had gone in to browse some of the old comics I'd bought and guarded so lovingly when I was a kid. One day, while tidying up my room, my mom gave them all to a thrift shop, and they sold for a nickel apiece before I could run down there to save them. A few months ago, when I looked in Just Dug Up Collectibles and saw the outrageous prices those issues were now selling for, I left the shop in despair and never went back.…

"Is there anything else I should know? Anything that might help?"

The Tannenbaums looked at each other, as if uncomfortable, hesitant, then both shook their heads.

Sheyenne whisked in and made several color photocopies of Buddy's photo before returning the snapshot to Mr. Tannenbaum, who lovingly tucked it back into his wallet. "I'll also submit this to the Talbot & Knowles blood bars," Sheyenne suggested. "They can include it with the other photos of missing children."

Mr. Tannenbaum looked uncomfortable. "I'd prefer to keep this out of the public eye."

"We already talked to the blood bars," snuffled Mrs. Tannenbaum. "They said they were overbooked for the next two months until … until …" She began sobbing.

Mr. Tannenbaum completed the sentence. "Until Christmas." He patted his wife on the shoulder. "Please find him soon, Mr. Chambeaux. We have very important Hanukkah traditions, and Winter Solstice, too."

She sniffled again. "The holidays just won't be the same without our dear Buddy. Please find him, Mr. Chambeaux. Such a dear, dear sweet boy."

6

"That kid is an unholy terror!" said Adric the comic-shop owner. He barely glanced at the picture of Buddy Tannenbaum. "He and his friends are monsters—and I don't mean that in a good way."

The wall behind the counter was plastered with autographed 8 × 10s of Adric posing with D-list celebrities. He was a gray-skinned, pot-bellied zombie, not nearly as well-preserved as the special variant-cover issues he kept bagged-and-boarded on high shelves. His complexion showed some signs of putrescence as well as fresh acne, which made him doubly unfortunate; although the undead suffer from numerous physical maladies, few are afflicted by zits.

Adric wore a powder-blue *Star Wars* T-shirt with R2-D2 and C-3PO on the front, and it was much too small for him. I deduced that he'd bought the shirt when he saw *Star Wars* first run in theaters; in the years since, his body had enlarged considerably, though he probably told himself that the shirt had shrunk.

Adric handed me back the photo. "That kid and his friends are always in here stealing things, vandalizing, harassing customers, and of course never buying anything. A bunch of deadbeats and undeadbeats."

I frowned. It seemed Buddy Tannenbaum was not the upstanding young werewolf his parents imagined him to be. "He's gone missing. When was the last time you saw him?"

He snorted. "I kicked out the whole wild bunch two weeks ago—caught them shoplifting one time too many."

I had another thought. "So, does that mean you keep a list of, say, who's naughty and who's nice?"

"Nah, this is a comic store. We get all kinds in here. That Buddy Tannenbaum and his friends, though—they'd definitely go in the Naughty column."

As he talked, Adric used a box-cutter to slice open a cardboard case of new arrivals like an eager coroner working on his favorite autopsy. He opened the flaps and began pulling out shrink-wrapped Christmas ornaments, clumsy-looking figurines of werewolves, vampires, scaly demons.

Frowning in disgust, he held up a crudely painted vampire with red marks smeared across his face. "Look at these! My customers want quality. The catalog said they're hand-painted, but this looks like it was finger-painted, or *claw*-painted." He shook his head. "Maybe even *flipper*-painted."

Adric dug into the box, pulled out a larger figure, a well-muscled werewolf in a cop uniform, holding an enormous Magnum pistol. "Does this look like Hairy Harry to you?" The rogue lycanthropic cop from the UQPD was something of a folk hero, even though he'd retired from the force.

"I wouldn't pay a premium for it," I said. I noticed the figures were labeled *Elfis Originals! Collect Them All!*

Adric kept pulling figurines out of the packaging, then rolled his eyes as he lifted out six genuine Elfis figurines, each wearing a white sequin jacket, brushed-back black hair and sideburns, and big sunglasses. "What? I only ordered one of these."

Next, he removed a larger box showing a scaled aquatic gill-man labeled "Special Limited Edition Creature! (Comes with free lagoon!)." With his stiff zombie fingers, Adric pried open the package, removed the scaly figurine along with a tiny black plastic basin. Apparently, the user was supposed to fill it with water.

"Special Edition? Ridiculous! Look at this: 'Limited to 1,000,000 Units.' How the hell does that make it *collectible?* I'll be lucky to sell six … well, five, because I'll keep one for myself."

I tried to get back to the reason I'd come there. "Have you seen any of Buddy's buddies? Anyone I could talk to? His parents are distraught."

"No, and good riddance. Maybe they all ran off to join the vampire circus." Adric continued setting out the Elfis Originals holiday ornaments. "Mark my words, his parents will have a lot more silent nights this way. Just imagine what a handful that werewolf kid is gonna be when he hits his teenage years and hormones kick in."

He looked up at where two young zombies were pawing over back issues of *The Crypt-Keeper's Funniest Capers*. The zombie teens had their mouths open and they moaned in laughter at the panels.

Adric yelled, "Hey, you! Be careful with those—you get decaying flesh on any of the pages, you bought it."

The zombies looked up at him, moaned, then went back to the comics, noticeably exercising greater care.

I picked up a fine-print catalog listing of the Elfis Originals ornaments and collectibles and pocketed it for future reference. I thanked Adric and left.

7

When Santa Claus returned to our offices, he looked even more anxious than before. His face was sallow, almost jaundiced; his flowing white beard looked scraggly, with a thin brownish stain from where he'd been hitting the pipe a little too often. He had lost enough weight that his red jacket was gathered in folds around his waist with his wide black belt cinched tighter. I saw that he'd even punched a new hole.

"Usually when I visit, people set out milk and cookies for me." He sounded disappointed, beaten down. "I'll be glad to get back to running the bed-and-breakfast, but I have my duties first. I can't do my rounds without that list of Naughty and Nice." He slumped into a chair beside Sheyenne's desk and let out a sigh. "I tried to write a new one from memory, but my mind isn't what it used to be—too many bitter cold nights out in a reindeer-powered sleigh. I won't kid you, Christmas Eve is a hard night—a real nut-cracker. After it's over, I crawl into bed and sleep for a week."

"My accountant says the same thing about Tax Day," I told him.

Santa adjusted his floppy red cap. "I haven't heard you jingle my bell, and time is running out. It's beginning to look a lot like a screwed-up Christmas."

"I've been investigating," I reassured him. "Particularly your rival Elfis. He makes no secret of the fact that he wants to take you out, but he insists he doesn't need your list to do it. What can you tell me about him?"

Santa's face fell, as if his heart had shrunk three sizes that day. "That elf deserves a lump of coal in his stocking on Christmas morning. Unfair business practices, inferior materials—do you know that his silver bells are made of cheap aluminum?" He frowned again, let out another sigh. "I try not to think ill of people, but I'd like to take a thick candy cane and go thumpety-thump-thump on his head. He's ruining traditions by taking away the incentive for children to be Nice. Just look at the rude manners in chat rooms on the internet."

My heart went out to him. "I'm looking into his North Pole South operations, and Robin is studying his business practices. I haven't found any evidence that he arranged to steal your Naughty and Nice list, but I'll keep digging."

After rummaging around in the kitchen, Sheyenne flitted into the main room, carrying a plate with three stale chocolate-chip cookies and a glass of milk. "Look what I found for you, Santa!"

He brightened. "'Tis the season to be jolly—so I'll try my best." He pulled a paper ticket from the pocket of his red jacket. "Could you validate this for me? I've got my reindeer and sleigh parked on the roof."

"Of course," Sheyenne said, and stamped his parking ticket.

Santa took the rest of the cookies "for the reindeer" and slipped through the door just as Mr. and Mrs. Tannenbaum hurried in. They looked anxious, and my heart sank, wondering how I was going to tell them that their darling Buddy wasn't the sugarplum they believed him to be. If the young werewolf was getting into so much trouble, how could the parents not know? Were they willfully oblivious to the fact that their angel came straight from the dark side?

"We weren't entirely honest with you," Mrs. Tannenbaum said, then looked away shyly. "We have something else that might help."

Her husband said, "I convinced my wife that we needed to give you every detail if we want our Buddy back. Our son is more important than our shame and embarrassment."

"We thought you might be able to solve the case without it, and then we wouldn't have to admit … admit—" Mrs. Tannenbaum's lower lip quivered. Her eyes flashed golden, and I could see a hint of werewolf coming to the fore.

"Buddy's given us difficulties before," Mr. Tannenbaum admitted. "He's an unruly kid. I think it comes from his full-fur blood. Trouble in school, trouble with vandalism. He's even run away from home a few times."

"But he always comes back," Mrs. Tannenbaum interjected. "He's a good boy at heart."

I asked, "Do you think there's any possibility that he's just run off again?"

Both Tannenbaums shook their heads. "Not so close to Christmas. He would have waited to get his toys first. He's a troublemaker, but he's a greedy troublemaker."

I didn't know if that was the best kind or the worst kind. "The information doesn't help a great deal at the moment, but I'll keep asking around."

The Tannenbaums looked at each other. "Oh, that's not what we meant to tell you, Mr. Chambeaux. We were reluctant to say anything about what we did because … because, well, it's not exactly legal."

That's never a good phrase to include in a sentence. I braced myself.

"We had to do something because Buddy ran away so often. So, the last time we took him in to the vet …" Mrs. Tannenbaum swallowed hard, then lowered her voice. "We had a tracking chip implanted in the base of his skull. Nothing anyone would notice, mind you, but … just in case."

I perked up. "A tracking device? Then we can pinpoint his location right away!"

"Yes," said Mrs. Tannenbaum. "Do you think that might help you find him?"

I slapped my forehead, and it made a hollow popping sound from the bullet hole there. "The cases don't solve themselves," I said, "but I do need all the information."

"The tracking signal has a very limited range," Mr. Tannenbaum said. "Quite discreet, but not terribly useful. Still, if you get close enough …"

The Tannenbaums looked sheepish after they gave me the secret frequency and serial number of the tracker. "Just bring our little boy home, please? That would be the best present we ever had."

8

When we began our search, I decided to take police backup—McGoo—just so I could say I was being sensible. I didn't want to go overboard, though, because there was a better-than-even chance Buddy had just run away with his juvenile delinquent unnatural pals. Still, if Buddy's disappearance was connected with the other missing kids, McGoo would want to be along.

Then Robin insisted on joining us. With such a three-pronged approach, how could we not be prepared to solve any problem?

She had frowned in disapproval when she heard about the implanted tracker chip, claiming that it violated the civil rights of an underage werewolf. But McGoo had seen enough troublemakers in his work, and he was more inclined to try the "terrified straight" approach. Robin finally conceded that if the tracker meant we could reunite the full-time fuzzy kid with his once-a-month fuzzy parents, then all was for the best.

With the tracker's frequency and serial number, Robin downloaded a free but highly rated Track Werewolf app for her smartphone. She bundled up in a wool coat, and we all set off into the snowy night to find Buddy, leaving Sheyenne in charge of the office.

We wandered around the Quarter for a frustrating hour, following false signals (a garage-door opener and a universal TV remote control). I was beginning to think that we might not pick up the tracker's limited-range signal until after we had already found the subject in question. We were lost and frustrated; what had seemed to be an easy solution was turning out to be a headache and a waste of time.

Then Sheyenne called us and saved the day. She had found an update for the Track Werewolf app, which dealt with certain bugs and user issues and increased sensitivity. Once Robin installed the update, we found a strong signal. We were closer than we thought.

The signal led us straight to the tall smokestacks and gigantic toy warehouses behind Elfis's North Pole South complex.

Holding her phone, Robin took the lead, guiding us along the chain-link fence to the back service entrance of the gigantic manufacturing warehouses. The temperature was dropping, and fluffy snowflakes drifted down. Not a creature was stirring, not even the ones that usually stirred at that time of night.

Approaching the back guard gate, we found two burly golems wearing security guard uniforms. Their clay bodies were stiff and hardening in the cold, but one perked up. "Do you hear what I hear?"

The other said, "Do you see what I see?"

Now alert, the golems prepared to block our way, both of them focusing on McGoo's uniform, the dark blue police shirt, trousers, and cap. "That looks good on you," said one of the golems.

"We both wanted to be cops, but couldn't pass the tests," the other explained.

I knew why, but I didn't embarrass them by pointing out the reason.

McGoo said, "We're searching for a missing child, and we have reason to believe he's inside one of the warehouses." He held out a copy of Buddy's picture.

"Kids just can't stay away from toys," said the first golem.

Robin held up her smartphone, showing the app. "And we have electronic evidence he's in there."

The golems were again intrigued. "Is that phone one of the new models?"

The other said, "Does it have Angry Vultures on it? Or Curses with Friends?"

I knew if the golems started playing games on Robin's phone we would never get past the gate. "We need to have a look, bring that boy back to his parents."

The first golem had a stony expression on his clay face. "Sorry. We can't let you inside. Elfis is very strict."

The other golem looked intimidated. "He sees you when you're sleeping, he knows when you're awake, he knows when you've been bad or good." In tandem, they shook their smooth clay heads and pointed upward. "Security cameras."

Time for Plan B. I removed a folded sheet of paper from the inside pocket of my jacket and showed it to the two golems. "We have a duly authorized search warrant to enter the premises, signed by Judge Hawkins herself. This grants us unfettered access to all parts of the North Pole South warehouses so we can find and rescue the young man."

The first golem guard took the sheet of paper and studied it intently, while Robin shot me a questioning glance. She craned her neck to see what the guards were looking at. McGoo could barely keep the smile off his face.

The other golem took the sheet from his partner; they both had frowns on their clay faces. "All right then. We're security guards, sworn to uphold the law." They opened the chain-link gate for us. "Go on inside. I hope you find what you're looking for."

Robin was perplexed, but she glanced down at the blinking light on her Track Werewolf app. Buddy was definitely close, inside the big factory building ahead of us. With his best I'm-an-authority-figure gait, McGoo marched away from the guard golems. Robin hurried alongside me. When we were out of earshot, she asked, "What was that all about? When did you get a search warrant?"

"It wasn't a search warrant," I said. "It's the fine-print listing of Elfis Originals I took from Just Dug Up Collectibles."

McGoo worked at the warehouse door; it was unlocked. "Golems can't read," he said. "At least most of them can't. That's why they couldn't pass their UQ Police Department exams. Good work, Shamble."

Robin was astonished. "Then we got in here under false pretenses, and I have real ethical problems with that. We're trespassing."

"We're rescuing a missing child," I said. My boundaries were a little more blurred than Robin's, but I did manage to get things done.

Robin was about to continue her objections when McGoo opened the loading dock door. The dark, noisy factory hangar was worse than the worst New Year's Day hangover. It was a true holiday of horrors.

9

I doubted children opening their gifts on the morning of Christmas Eve Eve (if Elfis and his minions delivered on time, as promised) would want to know where their presents really came from.

We were seeing the ugly side of holiday cheer: appalling labor conditions, thick smoke, clanging hammers, grinding gears, and jets of steam venting from pressure valves. Foul water trickled out of rusty pipes overhead. A labyrinth of rattling conveyor belts rolled toys along to packaging lines. Sparks flew and blazing fires roared out of open furnaces fed with black coal that poured from supply hoppers in the ceiling. A separate set of conveyors dumped defective metal toys into a smoldering furnace. It was as if the Island of Misfit Toys had an active volcano.

Robin looked around in horror, shocked by what she saw. McGoo's face was stormy with anger.

Most appalling of all, though, were the kids shackled to the assembly line, hunched over the conveyor belts, red-eyed, dirt-smeared, waifish. They toiled at assembling dolls, painting action figures, stuffing collectibles into boxes. There were werewolves, zombies, ghouls, even human children, all looking dejected and haggard.

As I scanned the faces, I recognized many of the kids featured on the Have You Seen Me? pictures from the Talbot & Knowles blood bars. I saw one gray-furred werewolf boy, mangy and yet somehow still cute, chained to a station where he was applying black button eyes onto Raggedy Ann dolls. Either he was confused by the instructions, or the dolls catered to an entirely different type of unnatural, because he sewed three eyes on each doll.

"That's Buddy Tannenbaum!" I said.

The boy heard me even over the factory din. He turned, his tongue lolling out of his mouth, and his eyes lit up upon seeing us. He dropped the doll onto the dirty factory floor and leaped toward us, but was brought up short by silver shackles that bound his wrist and ankle.

"I'll be good! I promise!" he yelped. "I won't be naughty anymore. I don't want to be on the list!"

Robin was ahead of us, grim and determined. "We'll get you out of here, Buddy. Your parents hired us to find you."

"My mom and dad? But Elfis said they didn't love me anymore."

"Of course they love you," Robin said. "Parents love even naughty kids."

A steam whistle blew. More coal dumped out of the feeding hoppers, and the furnace burned brighter.

Then the elves came—evil elves, and ugly enough that they might have been disowned by even the G-side of the family. They carried cattle prods painted like cheery candy canes; others brandished icicle spears that dripped in the intense heat of the factory floor.

McGoo and I drew our guns and stood next to Robin. The ten elves closing in didn't look afraid of us at all. Too late, I realized that they were just a distraction.

Two other hench-elves stood up from behind the conveyor belt and hurled snowballs at us—icy snowballs with rocks in the middle. Cheater snowballs. (I did say they were evil elves.) Their aim was supernaturally true, and with one hail of hard snowballs, they knocked the guns out of our hands.

Then the hench-elves closed in, wielding icicle spears and candy-cane cattle prods. They overpowered us, shoved us to the factory floor, and used tough strands of satin ribbon to bind our wrists. We were going to have a black-and-blue Christmas. An evil elf even slapped a coordinating stick-on bow on each of us before they herded us toward the back of the factory.

"Elfis is going to want to see you," said one of the guards.

"Oh, by gosh, by golly, that was on my Christmas wish list," I said, which earned me a jab from one of the cattle prods. Since I'm a zombie, it takes a lot to shock me, but the experience was still unpleasant. I was more worried about McGoo and Robin, who could indeed be permanently damaged.

Elfis was at a raised supervisor's station near the warmth of the big furnace, sitting on a high director's chair with a small worktable beside him. Black dust from the coal hoppers left a gritty film on everything, but somehow it didn't affect his white sequined jacket or his blue suede shoes. He was perusing a rolled parchment filled with names—countless names, sorted into two columns, one marked N and the other one marked N. He muttered to himself as he used a large goose quill pen to check off names.

"Naughty … yes, got that one. Naughty … yes. Naughty … we have a very high success rate." Then he sneered at a line, crossed it out vigorously with the nib of his quill pen. "Somebody slipped up—this kid's in the Nice column! People tend to notice when *nice* kids go missing." A supervisor hench-elf scurried off to rectify the error.

Elfis picked up a bullhorn and began shouting toward the factory floor. "Listen up, kiddies! I have plenty more applicants to choose from, so if you want to be promoted in my criminal organization, you've got to produce, produce, *produce!* Only the best can survive this boot camp—also known as the Holiday Season! If you work hard, you'll be real henchmen by Easter." Elfis then started to laugh. "We're going to put that damned bunny out of business, too!"

He slid his sunglasses up on the bridge of his narrow nose as his fiendish hench-elves pushed us forward. He seemed surprised to see us. "Mr. Chambeaux and friends—have you come to negotiate on Santa's behalf again? Well, it's too late. I've already got the holidays sewn up in a body bag, and now you'll never stop me."

When all else fails, when things look grimmest, I like to state the obvious. It puts villains off guard and usually gets them talking—too much. "You said you didn't have Santa's list of Naughty and Nice. That was dishonest."

He held up a long finger. "No, that was *misleading.* I said I didn't steal the list in order to earn brownie points or to make Santa look incompetent. I stole it strictly for my own purposes." Elfis waved the parchment, showing us the long list of names. "It's a recruitment tool, like a screening folder for job applicants. Santa already identified the *naughty* children for me, the ones suitable to become part of my operation."

"But you put them to work as slave labor," Robin said.

Elfis shrugged. "Well, they are naughty. Even criminals need to know the consequences of their actions. You do the crime, you pay the time. Community service for *my* community."

I struggled against the satin ribbons binding my wrists. It reminded me of my childhood, trying to snap the ribbons so I could open my presents. Now, as then, the ribbon had supernatural strength.

Elfis leaned forward, opening both of his hands to warm them at the nearby furnace. The conveyor belt continued to clatter, dumping defective toys into it, plastic ones as well as metal. "It's so nice to be warm for a change. And you three will be all toasty, too. I'm afraid I can't allow my plans to be foiled—or tinseled. Into the furnace with them!"

The hench-elves swept forward like a blizzard of evil. Even though I'm a zombie, I had no desire to be cremated. And speaking for my two human friends, I knew that neither Robin nor McGoo wanted to tour the interior of the furnace either. I had to get us out of there.

Zombies, for all of our fragile bodies and flesh that's prone to decay, have very strong teeth. Some zombies use them for ripping into flesh and bone; now I discovered that my teeth were excellent at cutting Christmas ribbon. I tore into my colorful satin bindings, snapped the ribbon—and I was free.

But I couldn't fight all those armed hench-elves. Thinking of only one thing that might save us, I jammed my hand into my jacket pocket and grabbed the loop attached to the emergency jingle bell.

It wasn't much of a jing-jing-jingle—but it was enough to summon Old Kris Kringle.

The flames in the furnace brightened, then made a coughing sound. Black smoke swirled out, and with a whoosh of hot air Santa Claus slipped down the smokestack and made his dramatic entrance. The conveyor belt came to a screeching halt as the jolly guy in the magic red suit (which also proved to be non-flammable) emerged from the furnace like something out of *The Lord of the Rings*. He planted his gloved hands on his hips and bellowed, "Ho-ho-ho! Who's been a naughty boy?"

Elfis nearly jumped out of his skin and scrambled down from the director's chair so rapidly that his sunglasses clattered on the floor. With the empty cloth sack over his shoulder, Santa stalked forward like an avenging angel—and not the type that goes on top of a Christmas tree. He spotted his lengthy rolled-up list on the worktable and seized it, holding it up like a baton. "You have gone too far, Elfis. And now you'd better cry, because Santa Claus is coming to get you."

The hench-elves were panicked. They dropped their candy-cane cattle prods and icicle spears and cowered. Their teeth chattered as if they had gone caroling naked on a cold winter's night and no one was offering wassail, or even hot cocoa.

Elfis tried to run, but Santa quickly caught up with him. I couldn't believe how fast the old bearded guy could move, but he had to have a secret power if he could hit millions of households around the world in a single night.

McGoo held up his bound wrists for me to bite the ribbons. Now *that* was showing a measure of trust! "Good plan, Shamble."

"I call it Santa ex-Machina." I picked bright green satin out of my teeth, then turned to free Robin as well.

Santa had cornered Elfis by the big coal hoppers, and the evil elf had no place to go. Santa didn't need any help, but I was part of this, too—and I had a bone to pick with anybody who wanted to throw me and my friends into a furnace.

Next to me, one of the cowering hench-elves still had a sack filled with the icy rock-filled snowballs. I grabbed one and hurled it with perfect aim, proving that not all zombies are disoriented and uncoordinated. My snowball shot struck the release latch on the coal hopper just above Elfis's head. The trap dropped open, and Elfis looked up just in time to see a black avalanche dump down on him. He was buried under lumps of coal.

Robin, McGoo, and I rushed over to Santa, who gazed with satisfaction at the mound in front of him. "Coal is what Elfis deserved ... although I'd hoped he would turn his life around if given the chance. Such a disappointment."

"You knew Elfis beforehand?" I asked.

Santa nodded. "He was one of my toy laborers, assigned to my workshop for community service, but he escaped, broke the rules of his North Pole parole. I was going to report him, but not until after the holiday season was over. It's a busy time of the year, you know."

We heard a groan, then a stirring. We moved the coal blocks away to reveal an Elfis now entirely covered in black dust. He plucked in dismay at his ruined jacket. "I guess I won't be having a *white* Christmas."

Santa unslung the sack from his shoulder, tugged it open, and strode forward. "Here comes Santa Claus."

Elvis scrambled backward when he saw the yawning sack. "No, Santa! Please! No!"

"Naughty children get what they deserve." Santa snatched Elfis, stuffed him into the sack, and cinched the opening shut. The captive kept squirming, but could not get out. Santa tucked his rolled up Naughty and Nice list under one arm. "Thank you all. I'll start checking these names, see who deserves to be sentenced to the North Pole for a few years."

"*Sentenced* to the North Pole?" Robin said.

"Oh-ho-ho, this list doesn't just show me who gets presents and who doesn't. The naughtiest of the naughty have to help me spread holiday cheer. Parents write me, too, you know. 'Dear Santa, please help me with my child who keeps acting out.' We have a community-service program up at the Pole, where naughty children can learn good behavior by doing good works." He had a twinkle in his eye. "There's a long waiting list, but our success rate is remarkable."

"Except for Elfis," I said.

"Some nuts are harder to crack than others, but a few days of shoveling out the reindeer stables usually makes them a little more cooperative."

Moving with supernaturally swift footsteps, Santa stalked around the factory floor, grabbing the cowering hench-elves one by one and stuffing them into his sack, which was obviously much larger inside than it was on the outside. It needed to be. How else could it hold a world's worth of toys?

With the bulging, squirming load over his shoulder, he turned to Robin, McGoo, and me. "I'll let you free the children." He turned to the shackled waifs on the now-still production lines. "Ho-ho-ho! Have you all learned to be nice instead of naughty?"

A chorus of the enslaved kids affirmed that they had indeed learned their lessons. Some, including Buddy, even volunteered to do community-service work up at the North Pole—after they recovered back home with their loving families.

Santa went to the coal furnace, shifted his heavy sack. "I won't forget you on Christmas morning, Mr. Chambeaux. Or you either, Ms. Deyer, or Officer McGoohan. And now, Merry Christmas to all, and to all a good"—he pushed down his black glove so he could double-check the time on his wristwatch—"a good night." He tossed the squirming bag ahead of him into the mouth of the furnace, touched the side of his nose, and vanished up the smokestack.

"Elfis has left the building," I said. "But the kids are still here."

The three of us spent the better part of an hour freeing the natural and unnatural children from their shackles. When Robin unlocked his chains, Buddy Tannenbaum threw himself into her arms. "Thank you, thank you! Can you take me back to my Mom and Dad now?"

"You'll be home for Christmas," I promised.

For a lot of families, it would be a happy holiday season, except perhaps for those who had ordered their gifts from Elfis Industries and were expecting delivery by Christmas Eve Eve....

While McGoo called for backup to shut down the factory and secure the crime scene, Robin took down names and developed a plan to reunite the kids with their parents. I called the Tannenbaums directly, and Buddy's parents rushed right down. It was a wonderful reunion, with the werewolf kid nuzzling his parents and promising he would be good.

10

It was Christmas morning in the Chambeaux & Deyer offices—and we found surprise gifts waiting for us, brightly wrapped in colorful paper with holly leaves and berries, wreaths, and little snowmen. Since we didn't have a chimney, Santa could only have delivered the presents by breaking-and-entering, but I wasn't going to press charges.

"Looks like Santa was true to his promise," I said.

Grinning, Sheyenne brought the gifts into the conference room. "If you can't trust Santa to keep a promise, who can you trust?"

I hadn't put anything on my wish list, but Santa Claus was supposed to know exactly what a person wanted or needed. I had to admit I was curious.

"You first, Robin." I nudged the thin, rectangular box with her name on it. As a lawyer, Robin tried to remain cool and businesslike, but I could see the sparkle in her brown eyes as she tugged the ribbon aside, and politely worked at the tape. When she couldn't get it unwrapped, she used a letter opener to slash the paper with all the finesse of a well-practiced serial killer.

Inside was a single yellow legal pad and a sharpened No. 2 pencil. Her excitement dimmed, though she remained smiling. "I can certainly use these. And not every lawyer gets to use a pencil and legal pad from Santa himself."

"There's a note," I pointed out.

Robin pulled a slip of holly-fringed stationery from behind the second yellow sheet, skimmed the hand-written note, then read aloud as her smile grew. "'I don't normally give magical gifts—I don't want to establish a present precedent, but I am so grateful for your efforts. After checking my list and the footnotes I made throughout the year,

Robin, I know that your work delights you more than anything else. This special legal pad will never run out of paper, and the enchanted pencil will take notes for you so you can have your hands and mind free to concentrate on your client. Ho-ho-ho, best, S.C."

Robin's smile was wide. "I can't wait to try it out!"

Excited, Sheyenne picked up the box with her name on it. She used her poltergeist abilities to undo the bow, pull the ribbon aside, and then, giggling, ripped the wrapping paper to shreds. She opened the box to find an envelope inside—with both our names written on it.

"It's something the two of us can use, Beaux!" With luminous fingers, she opened the flap of the envelope to find an embossed, official-looking certificate inside. "Oh! An all-expense-paid romantic weekend for us at the cozy North Pole Winter Wonderland Bed and Breakfast! Off-season only, it says."

"Now that has definite possibilities," I said, imagining a wonderful time away with my girlfriend. We would have to be creative to overcome the supernatural difficulties that precluded us from touching, but I was up to the challenge.

"Open yours, Dan." Robin handed me the very small box with my name on it.

Judging by the size, I thought it might be a new pair of cufflinks or a tie clip, but who was I to doubt Santa's wisdom or imagination? Zombie fingers are not the most adept at unwrapping small gift boxes, and Santa's elves had used way too much tape, but I managed.

I opened a hinged, velvet-covered box to reveal a small plastic cylinder labeled "Magic Lip Gloss. Use Sparingly." I wasn't disappointed so much as confused, not sure what Santa had been thinking. "Lip gloss?"

Sheyenne made a delighted sound and snatched the tube out of the box. "I think it's for me, Beaux—and that means it's for you." She popped off the cap, extended the lip gloss, and applied it to her widening smile. "A special film for my ghostly lips that might just allow a kiss…"

She leaned closer, but I told her to wait. "Just a minute, let's do this right." I slipped a hand into my jacket pocket and withdrew the wadded and prickly tumbleweed ball of the McMistletoe artificial substitute that Elfis had been trying to bring to market. I raised it up over my head. "This is supposed to be as good as mistletoe."

Robin was skeptical. "With all the quality that we've come to expect from Elfis Industries?"

Sheyenne's lips glistened invitingly from the magic lip gloss. Under the McMistletoe, she came very close, and her ectoplasmic lips brushed against mine. Yes, I definitely felt a warm tingle.

"I think it works just fine," she said.

Locked Room

1

When a harpy tells you to do something, there's no room for discussion.

As a zombie private detective, as well as a regular customer at the Ghoul's Diner, I had plenty of experience with Esther the harpy waitress. She had been a client of mine, seeking to get rid of a bad luck charm that a customer had left her as a tip for the awful service Esther usually provided (if "service" is a word that even applies in that situation.)

Esther had a hawkish face, a raptorlike demeanor, and a vulturelike personality. Her curled iridescent feathers looked like straight razors that had been mangled in a mail-sorting machine. With her glittering eyes, she could shoot a sharp glare at anyone who looked at her the wrong way, and Esther considered almost any way "the wrong way." Her mood swings were best measured on the Richter scale.

Nevertheless, she was a client of Chambeaux & Deyer Investigations, and a paying one. In the Unnatural Quarter, where monsters tried to make quiet, normal lives for themselves, I'd had far worse cases before.

Late this afternoon, Esther had called our offices demanding—because Esther was incapable of making a mere request—that my ghost girlfriend Sheyenne and I meet her out in the Greenlawn Cemetery for the grand opening of a very special new crypt.

"It's imperative that you're both there," Esther said in a voice that made fingernails on chalkboards sound like sweet music.

As our office administrator, Sheyenne already knew about the case. "I'm surprised you want me along, too. Dan is our private investigator. I often help out on cases, but—"

The harpy cut her off. "Stop arguing with me! I need a zombie and a ghost. Be there."

We'd had a quiet day wrapping up cases and waiting for new ones to walk through the door. Robin Deyer, my human lawyer partner, had left town to visit her parents for their anniversary celebration, so it was only Sheyenne and me in the offices. I wouldn't normally leave the place unattended, but I had my phone and I didn't expect this would take long.

Besides, who was going to tell Esther she couldn't have what she wanted?

The Greenlawn Cemetery was a nice place, as far as cemeteries went, with well-tended lots, mid-range tombstones, and used crypts for rent or for sale. The flowers were replenished regularly, and a park and recreation area for new tenants had been added as part of an urban beautification project. After being killed during one of my cases as a human detective, I had been buried here, and then I clawed my way back out of the earth, cleaned myself up, put on a change of clothes, and got back to work. Yes, this place held fond memories....

As Sheyenne and I arrived at the cemetery, I wore my usual sport jacket with its stitched-up bullet holes and my traditional fedora, that didn't quite go low enough to cover the exit wound in the center of my forehead. I looked fairly decent—maybe even handsome enough to accompany my vivacious blonde, blue-eyed ghost girlfriend. Sheyenne drifted along beside me through the lanes of tombstones, ectoplasmic and glowing, too beautiful to touch (which was a good thing: since she was a ghost, I couldn't touch her anyway).

We found the harpy standing next to the impressive new crypt, which looked like a private fortress with thick granite walls and massive columns that conveyed an ornate but unwelcoming appearance. I wasn't surprised to see a broad-shouldered and bare-chested minotaur standing next to Esther. Yes, the classical architect would want to be there for the grand opening of his special new tomb.

With a loud snort, Percy Minotaur, Sr. adjusted the golden ring through his blocky nose. "Thank you both for coming."

The door to the crypt was wide open to show an austere, cold interior, dimly lit by high narrow windows.

"Where is everyone else for the celebration?" Sheyenne asked.

"We only need you two," Esther snapped, and gestured with a feathered arm. The harpy had an odd and unsettling feminine appearance, a sexiness that at first attracted men, then made them ill as they realized exactly *what* they'd been attracted to. "You're here to test Elspeth's tomb. There's no time to waste."

"How is your sister's condition?" I asked. "Any change?"

"No, still terminal." Esther sounded disappointed. "And still no closer to it."

The minotaur invited us through the open door of the tomb. "Allow me to show you the finer points of the new construction. It is magnificent, as usual."

Sheyenne and I entered the tomb, though there wasn't much to see—an open empty vault with stone walls, stone floor, stone ceiling. The narrow slit windows at the top of the wall were thickly barricaded. The harpy's hard face curled in a smile as she saw me looking at them. "Those are so my undead sister can look out like a sad kid on a rainy day … if she ever dies, that is."

The tomb walls glistened as if coated with some kind of thick varnish … or maybe saliva. "A special anti-ectoplasmic preventive coating," said the minotaur architect. "One of the special upgrades Esther requested."

In the center sat a raised slab on which the resident's body would lie in repose. "Is this where you'll place your sister's coffin?" I asked Esther.

"Coffin? Hell, no! Why buy a fancy coffin? Who's going to see her in here anyway? She can just lie on the slab."

"I take it that's why you didn't waste money on interior decorating, either?" Sheyenne asked.

"Why would I waste money like that on Elspeth? This damned crypt is already costing enough arms and legs to make a body-repair shop happy! And it's all his fault." She snorted at Percy, who snorted right back.

"Great work doesn't come cheap," said the minotaur. "This crypt is my finest creation so far. It is beyond a masterpiece, because I've already produced a masterpiece, and that's just a beginning. Elspeth's tomb will be—"

Esther cut him off, "Will be *serviceable*, I hope."

"It looks secure," I said. "Impressive."

"We'll see about that," said Esther.

She and the minotaur slipped back outside the crypt, and before Sheyenne and I could ask any questions, the minotaur flexed his muscles and swung shut the massive door.

The harpy had just enough time to say, in her shrieking voice (which could cut through stone blocks), "I sincerely hope you never get out. Ever!"

After the slab sealed, we heard the loud clang of the massive bolt slamming into place.

2

When the harpy had first contacted us about her sister's ailment, I couldn't be sure if she was angling for sympathy or something else. She preened herself in front of Sheyenne's desk. "Elspeth is dying, and she's been doing so for a very long time—an unconscionably long time!"

"Oh dear," Sheyenne said. "I'm sorry to hear that."

"Don't be sorry for her—be sorry for me! I've had to put up with all this."

Esther's sister suffered from a debilitating mange—a lingering illness that made her linger … and linger … and linger, like something out of a heart-wrenching movie of the week, but not at all poignant. Esther had been tending her, reluctantly, for some time.

"Elspeth was obnoxious even on her good days—I got all the charm in the family." Esther clacked her teeth together and curled her fingers so that metallic black talons extended from the tips. The harpy family must not have gotten a large share of charm to start with.

"Eslepth won't let anyone see her because the mange makes her revolting. I told her no one would notice, because she was revolting before she caught the disease—but she doesn't believe me."

"You certainly have a bedside manner," Sheyenne said.

Esther fluttered her feathers. "I always wanted to be a doctor, except that I can't stand sick people. They're so needy."

I wished Robin were here, because she was always good at handling difficult clients. "Is the mange contagious?" I asked.

"Always thinking of yourself, Mr. Chambeaux!" Esther snapped. "You have nothing to worry about—zombies can't catch it."

"Actually, I was thinking about you," I said.

Esther flapped her arms, extended her plumage, inspected the small pinfeathers in her underarms. "What, do you see any symptoms? I douse Elspeth with bleach every day, as therapy—but if she's infected me, I'll pluck her naked, then tar and feather her all over again!"

I tried to calm her. "Just asking a question. I didn't notice anything in particular."

Sheyenne turned on the charm, which I knew hid her acid annoyance. "And how can we help you at Chambeaux and Deyer Investigations, ma'am?"

"I'm having a new tomb constructed for my sister, a special monument with many added features, designed to my exact specifications. I've got to make sure it's done on time—and properly. There's no room for error."

She withdrew blueprints and spread them on Sheyenne's desk, unceremoniously knocking aside the other papers and folders for our pending cases. As far as Esther was concerned, no other pending cases were as important.

"I've hired the greatest architect to build thick walls, reinforced windows, and an unbreakable door, with a few external decorative flourishes that will make the tomb fit in with the other ones in the cemetery. They have covenants for landscaping and exterior design."

Looking at the blueprints, I was impressed. This massive structure would certainly stand out among the ostentatious crypts and memorial markers at Greenlawn Cemetery. I understood what she was thinking. "It'll be like the great pyramids of Egypt."

Esther snorted. "No—more like Alcatraz. Once I'm finally rid of my sister, I'll seal her up inside there. If she stays dead, then fine—but a lot of people don't stay dead anymore."

Since I had come back as a zombie and Sheyenne came back as a ghost, I said, "Yes, we're well aware of that."

The harpy strutted about our offices. "Elspeth is just too mean to stay dead. Once she goes, I don't want to deal with her anymore. If and when my sister comes back, whether as a zombie or a ghost, I want her sealed up where she can't bother anyone again. *Ever.* So, I have to be sure that tomb is undead proof." Her eyes glittered at me and Sheyenne. "That's where you two come in."

3

A private investigation agency has to take cases of all kinds, but some are more unpleasant than others.

We were sealed inside Elspeth's fortress-like crypt, but I had no intention of staying there. As Sheyenne drifted in front of me, her faint glow illuminated the austere vault. Her blue eyes sparkled, and so did her smile. "It's not so bad, Beaux—we're getting paid to be alone together in a very private place."

"I'd rather take you to a coffin-and-breakfast of our choosing." I walked to the solid stone door, pressing my hands against it, tentatively using my strength. I knew it wouldn't be easy to break out of the tomb, but I had to start somewhere. I pressed hard, felt no movement—the old immovable object and irresistible zombie conundrum. I felt around the crack with numb fingers, but couldn't find any latch or self-release button on the door.

Partly due to Robin's recent legal efforts, laws had been passed requiring all crypts to have emergency-release locks, since you never could tell when someone might wake up and need to get out. But Percy the minotaur had not built this tomb to code.

I pounded on the door, hard, but that did no good. My cold flesh didn't even make a satisfying thump. I wondered if Esther and Percy were still waiting out there, amused, trying to see how quickly we could escape from this trap.

"If you're that anxious, I'll just slip through the wall, undo the latch, and open the door," Sheyenne said. "It's handy to have a ghost around."

She drifted in front of me, gave me an air kiss. As a traditional ghost, she could flit through any solid object, and her poltergeist abilities allowed her to manipulate inanimate objects.

She gathered speed as she headed toward the stone wall. Normally she would've melted right through without a sound; instead, I heard an alarming wet *smack*, and Sheyenne's beautiful form flattened out as she pushed and pushed against the stones. It was a very strange sight. I heard a thrumming as she continued to push, growing more and more flustered. Her form was distorted into a strange blob-like female outline, plastered against the impenetrable wall. Finally she withdrew, recomposed herself, and hovered in front of me, shaken.

"That's not what I expected," I said.

Sheyenne ran her ghostly fingers on the surface. The glistening coating sparkled faintly with an afterwash of her spectral impact, and I remembered the protective film that the minotaur architect had applied throughout the interior of the tomb.

She sighed. "Maybe this case is going to be more difficult than we thought."

If Esther's sister came back from the dead, she would return as a zombie or a ghost; therefore, Esther had instructed the architect to design a tomb that was proof against either one. A ghost harpy sounded even more unpleasant than an everyday harpy. And a *zombie harpy* ... well, I didn't even want to go there.

Zombies were strong and persistent, but it wouldn't be hard to build thick enough barricades to contain a shambler, even a well-preserved one like me. A ghost was more difficult to contain permanently, but this new anti-ectoplasmic film seemed quite durable and effective.

"Esther must really be worried about her sister harassing her from beyond the grave," I said.

With increasing persistence, then frustration, Sheyenne flung herself against different walls of the crypt, then the ceiling, even the floor, but she couldn't get through. She drifted up to the narrow windows, hoping to find some chink there, but the reinforced panes remained sturdy. The anti-ecto coating was everywhere.

When hiring us to break out of this unbreakable crypt, we hadn't established any kind of time limit. That was my fault for not thinking through the parameters. Robin always chastised me for entering into agreements without my lawyer partner vetting them first. Live and learn … or, live, die, come back from the dead, and still miss the point.

I yanked on the raised stone coffin slab, and Sheyenne stood on the other side using her poltergeist powers, hoping we could uproot it, topple it, find a loose floor tile or something. No good. The slab and its base remained as sturdy as a redwood tree.

I removed my .38 from its holster, and Sheyenne looked at me, puzzled. If I fired the pistol, any bullets would just ricochet around the walls, but I had something else in mind.

I use the butt of the weapon to hammer the saliva-like varnish, pounding and pounding, but the film remained smooth, unscratched. "I was hoping to make a dent, chip away enough so that you could work your way through a chink in the armor."

She pressed her ghostly hand where I had been hammering, but couldn't find the tiniest nick. That stuff was tough!

Thinking the windows might be more vulnerable, I pressed up against the wall, reached as high as I could, and grasped the narrow sill. Pulling myself up, I raised my other hand and pounded on the glass with the .38. Again, the glass was armored, and the anti-ecto coating too thick. I didn't make a dent.

Back on the floor again, I tried to think the problem through. The cases don't solve themselves, but even with a hole in my head I can usually figure out a puzzle.

"Ah, of course!" I reached into the pocket of my sport jacket, removing my phone. "I'll just call somebody to get us out of here."

"That's probably cheating," Sheyenne said.

"The case agreement didn't preclude it."

Robin was far away and wouldn't be back in the Unnatural Quarter for days, but I had plenty of other friends in the Quarter I could call—particularly, Officer Toby McGoohan from the UQPD, my best human friend. I just needed to get him on the phone, and we'd be all done here tonight.

The phone said No Service. Of course. Esther and Percy would've thought of that and put in shielding. These days, almost everyone elected to be buried with a phone handy.

I sat down on the stone slab. "I hate to admit it, Spooky, but I think we're stuck."

4

Early in the case, Esther insisted that we meet her architect, as if we were challengers in a grudge match.

Percy Minotaur, Sr. was well respected in his field, not just in tomb design, but he had also studied with a man who claimed to be Houdini's ghost, working on a contract job for the Unnatural Quarter's prison system. Houdini's ghost and Percy developed specialized unbreakable prisons and holding cells for various unnaturals, demons, specters, and the like. Eventually Houdini's ghost was exposed as a fraud, that he was actually *Jim* Houdini, no relation whatsoever to the legendary magician. Jim Houdini was arrested, but before he could be brought up on charges, he had miraculously escaped and still remained at large.

Percy the minotaur's work, however, was quite remarkable. He had accepted Esther's commission to build an inescapable, unbreakable tomb for her sister, just in case. He seemed to relish the challenge.

Upon first meeting the bare-chested Percy, I asked him why he insisted on remaining shirtless all the time. Sure, he had a broad chest and decent biceps, but he wasn't going to win any Mr. Unnatural America contests, especially with a paunch showing over what should have been washboard abs.

The minotaur reached up to touch his big blocky head and his wide set of curved bullhorns. "Because of these. I can't ever pull a shirt over my head."

That made perfect sense, I supposed.

"How about something that buttons down the front?" Sheyenne suggested. "Maybe a nice Hawaiian shirt?"

Percy seemed embarrassed. "I never thought of that."

Esther stood in the architectural offices, impatient. "On with it. Just show them your portfolio." The minotaur displayed and explained photos of other buildings he had done, the façade of the Metropolitan Museum, several impressive tombs.

"My aim is to become the most respected, most widely known minotaur architect in the entire Quarter. I'm very bullish on my career."

He had spent a summer sabbatical at Notre Dame, considering how to create a fusion of Gothic cathedral architecture with typical Unnatural Quarter buildings.

"A developer wanted me to design tract homes in a new subdivision, but I would never stoop that low. A gated community is the minimum I would consider." With a fist he pounded his unspectacular chest. "My great works will endure the test of time. They'll last for millennia, like the pyramids."

"As long as they can endure a pissed-off undead harpy," Esther said. "That's all I care about. Better hurry up and finish the building."

"How long do you think your sister has left?" Sheyenne asked.

Esther made a disgusted sound. "She's been at death's doorway for years and years, but she just stands there on the welcome mat. How I hate it when she lingers. I wish she'd get on with her death, so I can get on with my life." She pointed a talon at me. "Your case, Mr. Chambeaux, is to test out the new crypt. My architect is confident, but I don't believe anyone. I wasn't hatched yesterday."

"What exactly do you want us to do?"

"You'll be locked inside. If you can escape, then you get paid. If you stay trapped in there until Elspeth dies—and that could be years and years—then the minotaur gets paid."

5

I had heard grim stories of trapped undead who were left to tolerate an eternity of unending boredom: vampires given the Jimmy Hoffa treatment, sealed in a coffin wrapped with silver chains and then sunk at the bottom of a deep cold lake, where the poor bloodsucker had to lie there without even a book to read or a digest of Sudoku puzzles. Or zombies that rotted and fell apart, unable to move … but if the brain remained alive, did the inanimate decomposing pile of tissue just while away the hours pondering the meaning of life?

Now Sheyenne and I were stuck inside a sealed crypt. Nobody knew where we were, and the harpy certainly had no intention of letting us out.

Through the narrow windows, we watched night set in, then daylight again … and now night had fallen once more. Sheyenne's frustrated spectral glow was the only illumination to keep me company.

We'd been stuck in the tomb for more than a full day. After we had exhausted the first round of escape possibilities, neither Sheyenne nor I had any idea what to try next. Robin wouldn't come back to the office for another week. As soon as she found us missing, she would immediately know something was wrong, but she'd have no clue where to look for us.

Officer McGoohan would be concerned much sooner than that, but he wouldn't know where to look either. He'd file a missing monsters report, and he'd worry about me far more than he would like to admit—but that didn't mean Sheyenne and I were getting out of there any time soon.

For a while, Sheyenne let herself enjoy the quiet solace of the two of us together. We had all the makings of a romance to last throughout eternity, though I had never pictured our epic would all take place in a single room.

"Somehow I thought I'd have a more spectacular end than this, Spooky," I said as we sat together on the slab. "My first death was kind of embarrassing, getting shot in the back of the head in a dark alley, while trying to solve your murder." I had no reason to wear a fedora inside a sealed tomb, so I took it off, set it in my lap. "Now here we are, stuck, with no place to go, not even solving a case."

"You'll figure out something, Beaux."

"I suppose we can hope that Elspeth gives up the ghost soon, so they'll have to open up the crypt. But that's not the way I'd like to wrap up a case. After all my detective work, I never thought I'd be stumped by a locked-room mystery."

Sheyenne snuggled close to me so that her ectoplasmic body blended into mine. I wished I could feel something solid, but we took comfort in each other's presence nevertheless. Although death was no piece of cake, her afterlife hadn't been too bad. We had a good thing.

We reminisced about the times we had together, but I could tell she was growing agitated. Finally, Sheyenne flung herself at the film-coated walls and ceiling, again and again, becoming panicked. She smashed against the barrier, distorted her spectral body, then flew off to strike a different wall, trying to find some weakness in the protective film. She was like a moth, battering herself against a lamp.

I lurched to my feet and tried to catch her, but of course she slipped right through my grasp. I tried to calm her. "Hey, Spooky—let me think. I know you have faith in me, so let's work this through. Calm down."

"I don't want to be stuck in here anymore! I just want to get back to normal." Sheyenne slumped back on the slab and sat shuddering.

"Normal?" I said, cocking my eyebrow. "We have to break out of a sealed tomb that was built for a harpy by a minotaur, and then go back to work for a detective agency in a city full of monsters. Yes, let's get back to normal."

I worked my way around the sealed door again, looking at the corners, looking at the wall. Maybe I would notice a clue after all.

Sheyenne said in a depressed voice, "Looks like this tomb will stand the test of time, like the pyramids—just like that arrogant minotaur said."

"He's talented, I'll give Percy that. He did exactly what Esther hired him to do," I said. "But I didn't really see him as arrogant—just proud of his work. He intended for this crypt to be his masterpiece." Which was saying something, I realized, because we had looked at his architectural portfolio, all the great works he had already created. His masterpiece …

I sat up straighter, turned slowly around. An architect like Percy the minotaur took so much pride in his work—he would never leave a masterpiece unsigned. Esther wouldn't have let him make a big flourish, since she owned the crypt, had commissioned it for her own purposes. But Percy … I was sure he would have found some way.

"Let's look for initials," I said. "Comb every block. If that architect is the artist I think he is …"

Sheyenne didn't let herself show too much hope, not yet, but she flitted to the ceiling and scrutinized the stone crown molding, while I methodically—or as is fitting for a zombie, *relentlessly*—went from block to stone block, studying each one, looking for a signature or initials, hoping I'd find what I needed.

Finally, on a floor tile in the corner, back behind the coffin slab designed to hold the harpy's body, I discovered it. "Found it!"

The ghost swooped over, hovering next to me so that her lambent glow illuminated the initials: PMS.

"Percy Minotaur, Senior," I said.

"PMS," Sheyenne said, "could well be Esther's initials. But what good does that do us?"

I ran my fingers over the initials and felt the roughness. If my heart had been beating much, my pulse would've sped up. "Percy chiseled his initials in here at the last minute. He must have slipped in, pounded the letters, and then left before Esther could spot him."

With a fingernail, I tapped the chiseled letters, found a noticeable nick. "And he carved them right through the ectoplasmic protective film. The barrier is broken here, a chink in the armor." I smiled up at Sheyenne. "I've seen you slip through a keyhole when you needed to. Can you get through this crack now?"

She brightened—literally. "Even if there's only a little slit, I'll make it work."

Sheyenne bent over, concentrated, and extended her finger, sliding it through the tiny chisel mark of PMS. The rest of the crypt was sealed to her with the anti-ecto film, but she managed to push her spectral form into that tiny crack.

Her finger went first, elongating, then her entire hand plunged after it. She was gathering speed. "I can do this, Beaux." She flashed me one of those beautiful grins until she spun down and dove entirely into the chiseled letters. She disappeared through the floor tile with a faint *pop*, and her spectral light went out in the crypt, leaving me all alone in darkness.

Until she used her poltergeist powers to throw open the heavy bolt that sealed the door, cracking open the entrance to the crypt. I pushed as hard as I could, shoving open the stone barricade. I worked my way out into the humid miasma of the cemetery night.

Sheyenne was there waiting for me, smiling in triumph. I inhaled a deep breath, and it smelled like roses.

6

Proud and satisfied, Sheyenne accompanied me as we presented our bill to Esther the harpy for services rendered. Sheyenne insisted on carrying the paperwork herself. Somehow, I don't think she liked the harpy much....

Esther was meeting with Percy the minotaur inside his offices, going over landscaping concepts and shrubbery arrangements for the exterior of Elspeth's tomb. Esther was never in a good mood, but right now she was particularly unhappy to see us. Instead of welcoming us back, instead of graciously accepting defeat, her bird-bright eyes flashed like black lasers. She whirled to the minotaur, shrieking. "You miserable failure!"

"Now there's no need for that, Esther," I said. "You hired us to test the tomb. I'm sure he can make modifications." I wasn't sure I wanted to suggest improvements, though; no matter how awful Elspeth was—and harpies had their own separate category for "awful"—no one deserved to be sealed away like that for eternity.

"No! I want him to start from scratch and do it right next time—and I'm not paying you until it's perfect."

Percy snorted so loudly that the gold ring in his nose flapped and jangled. "This is bull!"

Sheyenne slapped our bill down in front of the harpy. "We, however, expect to get paid. We did exactly what we were contracted to do."

Esther shrieked, "You'll get paid when—"

"We'll get paid *now*, thank you," Sheyenne said. "You can take it out of your tips at the Ghoul's Diner."

Esther always provided abominably bad service, but she was so intimidating that customers were afraid *not* to leave a tip.

With a huff and a squawk, the harpy found a purse somewhere among her plumage and paid us. "This has been a lousy day. My sister suffered a relapse."

"Sorry to hear that," I said. "Is she getting worse?"

"No, a relapse of *health!* Looks like she might last after all.... This is the worst day of my life. And they keep getting worse and worse."

"There's always tomorrow," Sheyenne said in a flippant voice, and she drifted out of the minotaur architect's offices, with me following her.

As I closed the door, the harpy was launching into a long succession of nagging instructions, but this was no longer my case. "We should make it a general practice not to take harpies as clients."

"Sure, there were problems, Beaux," Sheyenne said as we headed through the bustling, colorful, and unnatural streets of the Quarter, "but I did get to spend time with you, and I like cases like that."

I stuck out my elbow, and she slipped her ghostly arm through mine. It was a charade, but we were good at it now. As we strolled along, other naturals and unnaturals saw how we were both positively glowing. They smiled at us, and we smiled back.

It was a good day to be alive, but, barring that, it was a good day for us to be together.

The Writing on the Wall

1

"That zombie wrote *FU* right there on the side of my store!" said Howard Snark, the human proprietor of Stakes 'n Spades, the only full-service hardware store in the Unnatural Quarter. He put his hands on his hips and fumed as he stared at the dripping spray paint.

Howard was normally a pleasant, soft-spoken man with salt-and-pepper hair, a full salt-and-pepper beard, and a salt-and-pepper personality. Standing there, I adjusted my fedora and inspected the graffiti. I could understand why he was upset, since his store had been defaced, but I thought he was misinterpreting.

"Actually, I think it says *FA*, Howard," I said. As a zombie detective, I have to pay close attention to details.

Beside me, my partner Robin leaned closer and nodded. "Dan's right. It's *FA*. Zombies don't have the best penmanship." She sounded apologetic.

We all stood together outside Stakes 'n Spades responding to the complaint, along with Officer Toby McGoohan, or McGoo. While walking his beat, he had apprehended the zombie tagger right as he was scrawling the letters with a can of lime green spray paint.

"It's still a violation," said McGoo, "regardless of the spelling."

The zombie graffiti artist looked dazed and confused, staring perplexed at the spray paint can in his grayish hands, as if he couldn't remember what he'd been doing.

Howard snatched the can away. "What were you thinking, Eddie? You're one of my regular customers. What did I ever do to you? I'm just trying to make a living here."

Howard had opened Stakes 'n Spades in the Unnatural Quarter because he saw an unfulfilled need. After all, monsters needed plumbing equipment, tools, lumber, nails, duct tape, and other building supplies as much as anyone else did. He had once lived in Silicon Valley, where many of his friends and colleagues became successful millionaires by working in software. Howard, on the other hand, had a vision that his own fortune lay in *hardware*.

When a rich, old aunt died and left him a modest inheritance, Howard built his store in the Quarter. Then, after he'd spent the entire inheritance, the rich, old aunt came back as a ghost and demanded some of the funds back. It could have been an inter-family argument with many consequences—legally speaking, the undead could sometimes reclaim their material wealth, depending on the amount of vagueness in the deceased's last will and testament—but, Howard and his aunt reached an amicable settlement. He gave her enough money to go on a retirement cruise with other ghosts, and he downsized his store slightly, but made it more profitable. Howard Snark had faithfully served the Unnatural Quarter for years, even becoming chairman of the Chamber of Commerce for a two-year stretch.

Now, McGoo stood with his report pad out, frowning at the zombie graffiti artist, ready to write a citation or make an arrest, whichever was necessary. "Well, Eddie, what have you got to say for yourself? You were caught red-handed."

Eddie looked down at his hands where some of the messy spray paint had covered his fingers in a neon-lime color. "I don't know."

He wasn't as well-preserved a zombie as I am, but he wasn't a horribly decaying shambler, either. His pants were slung low so that his waistband encircled the bottoms of his hips, while the waistband of his plaid boxer shorts was pulled high up on his back. Apparently, his demographic considers that sort of dress "stylish."

"What were you trying to write?" asked Robin. "FA … what else?"

"I don't know."

McGoo took off his policeman's cap and wiped a hand across his freckled forehead. His reddish hair was rumpled. "I don't know why these deadbeats can't just take an art class." He looked up at me. "Maybe you can solve this one for me, Shamble. There's been a rash of incomprehensible graffiti in the last day or two. None of it makes any sense. You're the detective—can you figure out what goes through a teenager's mind when he does stupid things?"

"That's beyond the skills of the most talented zombie detective," I replied. "And I *am* the most talented zombie detective—or so I've been told."

"That's what you tell yourself, at least," McGoo muttered.

"Did the other graffiti writing make sense?" asked Robin. When she decides to work on something, Robin is intense and dedicated. When she'd gotten her law degree, she decided to help the unnaturals who needed legal representation. She and I have been partners for a long time, both when I was a human detective, and now that I'm a zombie detective. When you have a good working relationship, you keep it.

McGoo flipped back through his pad. "First time, two days ago, some zombie just wrote *HE*—and then never went further." He looked at me with teasing scorn. "You zombies don't have a lot of follow-through."

"Some of us have ADDD. Attention deficit disorder of the dead."

McGoo looked down at his pad, turned the page. "Another zombie scrawled *I'VE* on a brick alley wall. Another one just wrote *LP*, whatever that means."

"I don't know," said Eddie again, even though we hadn't asked him the question.

"Maybe he was inspired." On the street corner in front of the Stakes 'n Spades hardware store sat a long-limbed zombie artist with a set of multicolored spray-paint cans and a stack of shiny hubcaps. Goch was a marginally popular street artist who specialized in painting designs on hubcaps, then selling them to curious human tourists who came into the Quarter to see everyday monsters in their natural habitat. Goch claimed that he "found" the hubcaps, although more likely, they had been stolen from parked cars. He had very long arms and legs that he folded up like a spider's, and long hair that made him look like an aging post-mortem heavy metal rock star.

Now, Goch held a spray can in his hand as he swirled a jet of color around on the hubcap. "When the muse takes you, you gotta paint."

"Well, he doesn't gotta paint *my store!*" said Howard.

Eddie slouched his head and his shoulders as much as his pants slouched. "I'm sorry, Mr. Snark … I don't know what came over me."

Howard let out an exasperated sigh. "Eddie, you're a good kid. All right, if you sweep up in the back, break down some boxes, and help run the store for a day or two, we'll call it even. I won't press charges—this time. I've got work to do. An entire new shipment of mallets and stakes came in, so we're having a special sale in honor of Bram Stoker's birthday."

Howard was always good at marketing.

McGoo put away his pad. "Doesn't bother me not to make an arrest. Less paperwork that way." He looked at me with gratitude. "I guess you didn't need to come out here after all, Shamble."

"We didn't come here for you," I said as Robin and I turned to go. "We're working on a case. We've been hired to see Angina, Mistress of Fright."

2

Despite her worldwide fame before the Big Uneasy, few people had seen Angina, Mistress of Fright since she'd retired from show business and become a recluse in the Unnatural Quarter.

She was a much beloved screamfest hostess, who had become quite a star on *Nightmares in the Daytime,* a monster movie double feature that had played first on a cable channel out of Chicago on Saturday afternoons before it caught on and spread around numerous syndicated channels.

With her scanty outfit, large breasts, and campy, as well as vampy, personality, Angina had become a cultural icon. Few people actually watched the bad black-and-white horror flicks she hosted; the audience was much more interested in her goofball comments, and her cleavage, during the breaks.

But when the breasts started sagging and crows' feet appeared around her eyes, Angina—whose vanity was legendary—retired from public life, preferring to be remembered as she was in her femme-fatale heyday.

Nowadays, though, with real monsters setting up shop and interacting with normal society, the demand for old horror flicks dwindled, so Angina had picked the perfect time to retire. And she found the right neighborhood for her retirement home.

Even though she chose the Quarter as her "unnatural habitat," Angina built high fences, barricaded herself in her house, and became a total recluse. She interacted with no one, had groceries and supplies delivered by golems who were sworn to secrecy. And she never left.

But recently an admirer, a dedicated fan, had engaged Chambeaux & Deyer Investigations to make contact with Angina. It was our job to make our client happy.

The Angina house was a rickety, bent-over affair (designed that way on purpose) with peeling wood siding, slatted shutters that hung askew on the windows, black shingles on the roof, a belfry complete with bats, seven gables close together. The house was surrounded by a brick wall topped by fierce-looking wrought-iron spikes and a dash of barbed wire (probably electrified). The rusty gate was padlocked shut. At the cornerstone of the brick wall, I saw the engraved notation, "Chas. Addams, Architect."

Everything about the Angina house looked rundown and dangerous—which was perfectly acceptable décor in the Unnatural Quarter, in accordance with the neighborhood homeowners' association covenants.

Just outside the padlocked gate I found a speaker and an intercom button. "Would you like to do the honors, Robin?"

I could see she was barely suppressing a giggle. "I confess, I'm a little nervous, Dan."

Robin had faced horrific monsters, fierce demons, and powerful black magic, but now she had butterflies in her stomach because she was actually a big fan of Angina, Mistress of Fright. She pushed the intercom button. "Hello?"

A loud, harsh, female voice burst out of the speaker. "Go away!"

"We're here to see Angina. We have a request—I hope you can help us out."

No answer—only dead silence.

My turn to push the button. "Is anyone there?"

"I want to be left alone!"

Robin's turn. She pushed the button. "We were hoping for an autograph, if it's not too much trouble."

"No trespassing!"

Robin and I looked at each other, and she seemed very disappointed. "A person has a right to privacy. We can't intrude if Angina doesn't want us."

Robin was always a stickler for the rules, which had worked much to our disadvantage many times. I've often found it more effective to apologize afterward than to ask her permission before I did any questionable activity.

I didn't give up so easily, though. "The cases don't solve themselves, and we have an obligation to our client to try everything possible. We've got to figure out a way."

Back at the offices of Chambeaux & Deyer, clients normally just walk through the door, whether it be a golem seeking justice for his comrades caught in an illegal sweatshop, or an opera-singing ogre who had lost his voice, or even human clients whose interactions with unnaturals hadn't gone well. (That happens more often than you might think.)

This time, though, we received our engagement letter via the mail. Jackson B. Hayes introduced himself to us as an avid collector, insisting that he was Angina's "number one fan!" Then he went on to reassure us that there was nothing obsessive about it, like Annie Wilkes of *Misery* fame, but that he really, really, really loved Angina. He had grown up captivated by her, watched every episode of *Nightmares in the Daytime* cinema, collected a Standee figure of her, posters on the walls. He had DVDs of her movies, VHS copies of her older ones, even Betamax copies of older ones still.

Jackson had sent us a black-and-white glossy photo, one of the beautiful head shots that showed Angina in her prime: alabaster skin and eyes with enough mascara and shadow to make an Egyptian sarcophagus jealous. The canyon of cleavage between her breasts was large enough and prominent enough that it could have been a national park, or at least a national monument.

"I desperately want to get this photo autographed," wrote Jackson. "It would mean so much to me."

So, he engaged Chambeaux & Deyer Investigations to break Angina's legendary reclusive barrier just long enough to get a signature. "And make certain it's an *authentic signature*. I've been duped before."

He described how he had purchased a signed photo from a collector on the internet, but because Jackson B. Hayes was an Angina expert, he recognized the forgery immediately.

"Angina always signed her autographed photos to her fans with a special exclamation point drawing the dot in the shape of a heart. She said it symbolized a stake going right into the fan's heart. So endearing! Since the photo I purchased had a normal exclamation point, I know it was fake."

Sheyenne brought the package to Robin and me. "Here's a new case."

"Sounds like an easy job," I said. "Everyone knows where the Angina house is."

Robin's eyes were sparkling as she began to gather our information, gazing at the beautiful black-and-white photo. "I'd really love to meet her myself."

I'd never seen my partner turn into a fangirl before. It was charming.

Sheyenne had used her poltergeist powers to dial the phone and let Jackson B. Hayes know that we would start work right away. All we had to do was get a minute of Angina's time.

Now, as we stood outside the imposing brick wall and padlocked gate, Robin clutched the black-and-white photo in its protective envelope. She wasn't sure what to do.

I pushed the intercom button again. "We won't go away until we see you, Angina."

The response came back loud and gritty. "Keep out! No trespassing!"

Robin pushed the button. "Please, we don't mean to be a bother, but—"

"I want to be left alone! Go away!"

This was starting to sound redundant. I pushed the button again. "Is this just a recording? Is there anybody in there?"

"No trespassing! Keep out!"

Robin looked at me, worried. "Maybe we could try again later. Perhaps a phone call? Send a package in the mail?"

"Zombies can be persistent," I told her.

"Not as persistent as lawyers," Robin said.

3

The Unnatural Quarter really got hopping after dark, when all the nightbreeds, vampires, and shadowy creatures felt their metabolisms rise. But it was after official business hours for Chambeaux & Deyer. I decided to relax with Sheyenne and watch a movie. Considering our Angina case, though, it was a work-related date.

Since my girlfriend is a ghost, she can't touch any living, or formerly living, thing, which makes it difficult to hold hands. She passes right through my flesh. But when she really gets into that spectrally romantic mood, she can don a polyester glove and make her grip feel almost lifelike. Since at times I can be almost lifelike, too, we make a good couple.

Sheyenne has been with me longer after death than we were a couple when we were both alive. Of course, our relationship and some unsavory acquaintances was what led to our respective murders in the first place, but neither of us let that dampen the post-mortem romance.

We sat in the conference room with a portable TV set and the lights turned down so we could watch a DVD of Angina, Mistress of Fright's *Nightmares in the Daytime*. The movie itself was an old stinker, *Revenge of the Grinning Skull,* whose effects were so bad the director must have gone home every night hanging his head in shame; the acting was so bad, the cast must have done the same; and the writing was even worse, so the screenwriter probably didn't bother to go home at all, for fear of facing his family once they'd seen the film.

But when Angina came on screen during the breaks, she was really something. The Mistress of Fright had a sparkle in her dark eyes, and she laughed so boisterously that sometimes her artificial fangs fell out—which she played for laughs, as well.

She groaned at a particularly awful point in *Revenge of the Grinning Skull*. "Angina must have gone out of her way to pick movies so bad that they would make her look good."

Her polyester glove levitated and I reached up to hold her hand. A fresh-popped bowl of popcorn sat on the conference room table in front of us, mainly for ambience, because a ghost can't eat and I usually don't have much appetite.

Normally, I would have gone to the Goblin Tavern to share an after-hours beer with McGoo, but that night I told him I had a date. "Must be nice, Shamble," McGoo had said. "You're dead, and you still get more girls than I do."

"Yes, that's me, McGoo. Always been a babe magnet."

"Me too. But I think my polarity is the opposite of yours. I just repel them."

McGoo was probably still walking the beat even this late at night; he didn't have much to go home for.

A few hours after Robin and I came back from our unwelcome reception at the Angina house, McGoo called to tell me that he had found more incomplete zombie graffiti scrawled on a wall in the Quarter. Another young zombie with the same intellectual capacity as Eddie had spray painted "*LLEN AND I*" before running out of steam.

McGoo had caught the deadbeat as he stood there looking at the can of spray paint in his hands. When McGoo demanded to know "Who's LLEN?" the zombie didn't seem to know. No surprise there.

Now, while Sheyenne and I watched the movie, Robin was burning the midnight oil in her office, poring over cases, studying legal precedents, writing up briefs. She's still alive but she doesn't have much of a life—except with us. I didn't want this talented young woman to work herself to death, but I knew that working on cases and hammering out briefs was how Robin chose to relax. She was more stressed when not working.

Robin came to stand at the door of the conference room, peeping in so she could watch the movie, too. "You're welcome to join us," I said.

She looked at Sheyenne and me holding hands. "I don't want to interrupt your date."

"You're not," Sheyenne said. "This is about as far as Beaux and I were going to get tonight."

"Always stuck on second base," I said.

Robin snagged the bowl of popcorn. "I will take this if you're not going to eat it. It smells delicious, fills the whole office."

She stood munching on a handful of popcorn, captivated by *The Revenge of the Grinning Skull*. "I remember this one!" When Angina came on, we all laughed aloud as a man in a rubber Creature from the Black Lagoon mask did pratfalls and fell into a half-full bathtub.

"Angina certainly has stage presence," Robin said. "With those looks, that body, she used to be quite a dish."

"And now she's just leftovers," I said. "No wonder she's a recluse."

Sheyenne said, "Maybe she just wants people to remember the way she was on screen. You never age there."

"Right," I said. "Like the Blu-Ray of Dorian Gray."

The phone rang. Even though it was after office hours, everyone knew that zombies and ghosts—and dedicated lawyers—worked all hours anyway.

Sheyenne flitted out of the conference room while I paused the movie. She didn't bother to use the door, simply passed right through the walls to get to her desk. Robin munched popcorn while we both listened to the phone conversation in the reception area.

"All right, McGoo, I'll send her right over. I'm sure Dan will want to come, too." After hanging up, Sheyenne flitted back to the conference room. "More trouble at Stakes 'n Spades. Goch, the hubcap artist, has been arrested, and he's demanding to see Robin as his lawyer.

I groaned. "What did he do?"

"Defacing private property, but he denies it. Said he's got to have Robin right away."

Robin set down the popcorn. "Sorry about your date and movie."

But Sheyenne understood. She always did.

4

It was the dead of night, but that's when the dead really got lively. At the hardware store, the streetlights were bright, and McGoo stood there flustered, disappointed, and at his wits' end.

Goch was in handcuffs, his long legs shaking so badly that his knobby knees knocked together. His colorfully painted hubcaps were strewn around, like a going-out-of-business sale for bad artwork. Several spray paint cans lay tipped over on the sidewalk.

Outside the hardware store, Howard Snark wrung his hands and shook his head. "I barely got the other graffiti cleaned off!" He shook his fist at Goch, who cringed. "Why can't you get a life?"

"Because …" said the zombie artist.

But Howard wasn't listening. "I am pressing charges this time, Officer McGoohan."

"I thought you might," McGoo said.

Scrawled in gigantic letters across the front of the hardware store, were the words "*CAN'T GET.*"

It didn't make any sense to me. "*CAN'T GET* what?"

Robin stepped up to the artist, using her most understanding voice. "You've got us all confused, here, Goch. What does it mean?"

The zombie heaved a long sigh. "You don't ask what art *means.*" He looked pleadingly at Robin. "It was the Muse—it must have been. I couldn't control myself. You have to defend me, Ms. Deyer. It's about artistic expression."

"I'd like to express myself all over your face!" Howard slapped his forehead. "I sold you that paint. I even bought four of your hubcap creations for my store—and this is how you thank me?"

When Goch trembled, his handcuffs rattled like the chains on a restless spirit.

Other unnatural spectators had gathered around—two vampires who had just come back from a nightcap at a Talbot & Knowles blood bar, a partially unwrapped mummy who was still in stitches from a show at a comedy club, and several slack-faced and curious-looking young zombies.

As Howard Snark and Goch continued to argue and McGoo wrote up the citation, one of the young zombie spectators shuffled forward, picked up a discarded can of pink paint, and walked over to the door of the hardware store. As we stared in disbelief, he started painting—right in front of us.

I lurched forward. "Hey! Stop that."

McGoo and I seized the arms of the disoriented young zombie who was moving listlessly like a … zombie. I grabbed the spray paint out of his hands.

He'd had time to paint the word "*UP!*" Oddly enough, the dot of the exclamation point was a cute little heart.

Howard groaned, exasperated. "What is wrong with you undead people?"

"*UP* with what?" Robin said to the dazed zombie. "You knew you'd be caught!"

"*UP* yours," Howard said. "You're going to pay to clean my building."

I paused and stared, though, looking at the words.

CAN'T GET and *UP!*

Then, I remembered the afternoon's new graffiti—*LLEN AND I*—and the incident that had called us here early in the day, *FA*.

The first graffiti McGoo had reported to me was just the word *HE*, but I recalled what else we'd seen. *I'VE* and *LP*. I was sure I was putting them in the correct order of how the graffiti had actually been written.

HE

LP.

"McGoo, it's a message. It all goes together. The graffiti is telling us something—and we'd better listen."

I felt a chill rush through my embalming fluid as I realized that the spray-painted letters spelled out that terrifying mantra so dreaded by senior citizens everywhere:

HELP, I'VE FALLEN AND I CAN'T GET UP!

"Who?" McGoo said, "Where? How do we respond to this? Shamble, you're onto something."

I pointed to the stylized exclamation point with the little heart. "It's Angina. And she's in trouble."

5

As we raced to the Angina house, I placed a phone call to Sheyenne. "Spooky, we might need you." She's always happy to help, and I seem to solve cases better when she's around. At least, that's what she says.

An emergency with a person potentially in peril took precedence over arresting a zombie vandal with a side career in hubcap painting.

Besides, we knew we could always find Goch again, since he was a well-known street artist, not a particular flight risk.

Howard said, "I'll hold Goch for you in the meantime. Stakes 'n Spades has a full line of chains, padlocks, and rope."

Robin, McGoo, and I arrived at the Angina house, which looked even more corny and stereotypical under the full moonlight. Sheyenne joined us just as we arrived; she's a powerful poltergeist who is not bound by the restrictions of physical travel as are human cops, determined lawyers, or shambling zombies.

Remembering the imposing padlock that held the main gate shut, I had planned ahead and asked Howard for a sturdy set of bolt cutters. He showed me the options from his store, gave me a sales pitch about the craftsmanship and the warranties of each. I just took the biggest one.

McGoo punched the gate's intercom button. "Ms. Angina, we're here to help. Are you in trouble?"

"Keep out! Go away! No trespassing!"

"Sounds like she's fine." McGoo lifted his eyebrows. "Though not very friendly."

"It's a recording," I said. "Same words every time."

"She's definitely in trouble," Robin said. "We've got to do something."

I grasped the bars to rattle the gate, and I was shocked, literally, when sparks crackled through my body. I yanked my hands away. Fortunately, zombies don't have to worry about being electrocuted.

"She means business," I said.

Robin sounded desperate. "Given the evidence, there's a reasonable expectation that this person is in danger. If it's to do a wellness check on a person who hasn't been seen in a long time, we have sufficient cause to break in. We're on sound legal ground here."

I lifted the tool. "And I've got a big bolt cutter."

"There's an easier way." Sheyenne took a shortcut by flitting right through the gates. "At least let me switch off the current."

Once through the wall, she deactivated the electrified fence, and I used the bolt cutters to snap the chain. We pushed open the gate and raced up the flagstone walk that was artfully surrounded with scraggly weeds.

Sheyenne vanished directly through the front door of the vintage haunted house. And, since my ghost girlfriend had just gone inside, it was now, quite literally, a haunted house—but in the best possible way.

McGoo, Robin, and I ran up the rickety wooden porch steps, and we heard a loud series of *thunks* as multiple deadbolts were turned. Sheyenne pulled the door open with a loud nerve-jarring groan and hovered in front of us, pale and glowing, but her expression was distraught.

"We're too late," she said.

I went inside first, with my hand on my .38 in its holster. McGoo had already drawn his service revolver, though there was nothing threatening inside the haunted house.

Just a dead body.

The foyer of the Angina house was a large receiving hall, with two towering grandfather clocks, ostentatious furniture, marble tiles, a dramatic curving staircase. And Angina, Mistress of Fright sprawled at the bottom of the stairs on the marble tiles. Obviously dead. And for several days from the looks of her.

Even though we had just watched *The Revenge of the Grinning Skull* on Angina's *Nightmares in the Daytime,* I barely recognized the famous horror film hostess. Angina had retired from the public eye and gone into hiding years ago. I suppose the kindest way to describe it was that she "had not aged as well as a fine wine." Angina had gained another film hostess's worth of weight, and her lush, black hair had gone gray and fallen out in clumps. Her skin showed numerous age spots (other than the normal discoloration of having been dead for several days).

"I guess we didn't have to run so fast."

Then the air above Angina's body shimmered, and a figure appeared—an indistinct and barely visible image of Angina, like the ghost of a ghost, a watermark in the air. She was just a flickering afterimage, compared to Sheyenne's bright and intense ectoplasmic form.

"It took you long enough!" She was indignant, but her voice sounded as if it came from a great distance. "Didn't you get my message?"

McGoo and I looked at each other. Robin said, "Not right away. It wasn't clear."

The ghost of Angina let out a disgusted snort. "Zombies are lousy messengers."

In sharp contrast to the decrepit old, overweight, and age-spotted corpse of the Mistress of Fright, Angina's ghost looked as if she had stepped right off of one of her pristine DVD images: beautiful face, voluptuous body, fine skin tone, and bodily curves that went gently in and out rather than just *out*.

"You're a ghost, just like me," Sheyenne said. "Don't you have poltergeist powers? Couldn't you just walk through the wall and get out?"

Angina's ghost let out a metaphorical sigh. "I tried, but I couldn't walk through walls, and I don't have any poltergeist powers. Looks like I washed out as a ghost, just like I washed out as a serious actress. I'm weak, and I'm trapped inside this house, but I feel that I'm supposed to move on. I needed help."

I made the connection. "So you possessed those zombies to put out your message."

"Zombies are very poor conduits, but they were the only thing I could use. Undead slackers—they're hard to control for more than a few minutes at a time."

I tried not to sound testy. "Some of us are well-preserved zombies."

"And a lot of them aren't well-preserved at all," Angina snapped. "It was an ungodly challenge to get them to write down one or two letters before their attention would wander off somewhere. The whole thing took days!"

Robin nodded solemnly. "Yes, ADDD."

"I couldn't leave the house, and I was stuck here, fading away, like my career. But at least you finally came."

"We were too late to save you, though." Robin frowned.

"Oh, don't worry about that. It was quick—I tumbled down the stairs, and … then I was a ghost. Besides"—she drew herself up, touched her breasts, ran her spectral hands along her spectral waist—"look at me! Quite an improvement, I'd say. That old body was quite a burden, and I'm glad to be rid of it. I like this much better.

"But after I died, I was trapped in this house, and I just couldn't figure out how to let anyone know." She glanced at Sheyenne, gave one of her signature Mistress of Fright winks. "Now, I may not be a poltergeist, but after all the movies I hosted, I remember damn well that ghosts can possess people—particularly weak-willed people. And who's more weak-willed than a zombie?"

I chose not to take offense at that.

"I just didn't realize it would be so tedious just to get one line right. Ugh, it reminds me of some of the actors I worked with."

"Well, we're happy to have found you now," Robin said. "We'll let you out of the house. Even as a ghost, you'll be welcome in the Unnatural Quarter. You'll fit right in. A lot of monsters watched your show, too. And …" She seemed embarrassed. "I'm a big fan, too."

Angina shook her faint, spectral head. "Oh, I'm not going out there! I need to move on. I know I do."

Yes, the undead had become a common sight—vampires, zombies or ghosts—but not everyone came back for an encore. Some people died and stayed dead … and they liked it that way. I was glad that Sheyenne had come back to haunt me, but Angina just felt trapped.

"Then I'm not sure I understand," I said. "What do you need our help for?"

"I died here alone, under violent circumstances. My body needs a proper burial before I can head toward the light."

"You sure that'll work?" McGoo asked.

Angina huffed. "Mister, do you know how many hundreds of horror movies I hosted? I've seen enough to know that's what you have to do."

6

The Quarter offered several services that could take care of Angina's needs, such as ghost-removal services and licensed "proper burial" teams with all the bells and whistles. There were budget plans and extravagant ones.

Angina, of course, needed to have the best.

Once released from her house, Angina had followed us out the front door, and now she hovered around the Chambeaux & Deyer offices, waiting as we wrapped up the details. Sheyenne described the ins and outs of being a ghost, but Angina wasn't really interested, since it wouldn't matter for long.

But I had other cases as well, and I always keep my clients' needs foremost in my mind. While we arranged for the proper disposition of Angina's corporeal remains, the real client who had started this whole mess—or adventure—was the autograph collector, Jackson B. Hayes. I wanted to wrap up that case while I had the chance.

I pulled out the black-and-white head shot that the fan had lovingly sent to us. "We were trying to get your autograph, Ms. Angina. That's why we visited you in the first place."

I showed her Jackson's letter, and faint fuzzy tears appeared in her translucent eyes. "I was always good to my fans."

"Is there any chance…?" I held up a pen. "An autograph would mean so much. Then we could close out the case."

Sheyenne drifted closer. "But if she doesn't have any poltergeist powers, Beaux, she can't scrawl her name."

"My penmanship was very neat," Angina said. "I would never scrawl."

"Maybe we could just get a photo of me holding up the glossy with you in the frame," I said. It was all I could think of.

Robin joined us. "She's very faint. I doubt the ghost image would even show up in the picture."

Angina, though, had a bright idea. "You're a zombie, Mr. Shamble. I could do what I did before. Hold onto that pen and empty your head of thoughts."

"That's easy enough for him," Sheyenne teased.

I couldn't let her get away with that. "Not when you're around, Spooky. I have lots of thoughts."

Robin was uncertain. "You want to possess Dan, so that he can write, just like the other zombies did with graffiti?"

"I can try," said Angina.

Whatever it takes to wrap up a case. I dutifully cleared my head, held the pen, and felt a strange presence enter through the bullet hole in my forehead, which was a very strange experience.

My hand moved of its own accord, flexing my wrist, limbering up, and then with a flourish I signed, "To my Number One Fan—Best Wishes, Angina, Mistress of Fright." For veracity, Angina possessed my hand and forced me to make the final exclamation point, complete with a cute little heart for a dot.

"There," Angina said. "See? A stake headed straight for the heart."

Robin witnessed the signature and signed a certificate of authenticity to verify for Jackson B. Hayes that Angina herself had autographed the photo. She also made a secondary notation that this was guaranteed to be the last signature Angina ever gave to a fan. Jackson would love that.

Within an hour, the proper disposal service had been completed, Angina waved farewell and then winked out of existence heading off to a better place where she hoped to find a new audience for her work.

After Angina vanished, I stood next to Sheyenne, who looked somewhat wistful. "I could've gone on at one time, but I stayed behind to seek justice, to find my killer … and to hang out with you, Beaux."

I didn't know what I'd do without Sheyenne. Unlife was so much better with her around. "You're not going to leave me, are you, Spooky?"

She smiled and snuggled close. I felt a tingle, but little else. It didn't matter, I knew she was right there, and her presence warmed my cold blood.

"No, Beaux. I'm here on purpose, and I intend to stay. We've got a lot more cases to solve."

Role Model

1

"Come on, Shamble—it'll be fun," said Officer Toby McGoohan, my best human friend. He acted as if he'd gotten season tickets to his favorite sports team.

I was immediately suspicious, sure that this would not be typical police business. "I don't even know what a cosplay convention is, McGoo."

He had met me outside the offices of Chambeaux & Deyer Investigations, seemingly by happy coincidence as he walked his beat, but we both knew it wasn't an accident. He'd been waiting for me.

"Cosplay—costume playing. It's when people dress up as characters from their favorite movies, TV shows, comics, video games, whatever." He had looked it up online, so he considered himself an expert.

"Oh. Trick or treat for grownups." Every day in the Unnatural Quarter, I saw a parade of werewolves, mummies, vampires, zombies, ghosts, witches, and second-string monsters, so I wasn't going to be impressed by a few interesting costumes.

"A lot more than that. These people think they *are* the characters. It gets a little intense. And weird. And fun."

It didn't sound any stranger than my usual cases, and McGoo and I often helped each other out. "So why do they need a zombie detective?"

He seemed exasperated that I was spoiling his fun by being such a hard sell. "They don't *need* a zombie detective any more than they need a beat cop, but the hotel manager is nervous about having such big crowds—naturals, unnaturals, all those people running around in costumes. Thought he might need some extra security." McGoo flashed one of those grins that had, over the years, convinced me to do things that would get us both in trouble. "Besides, he gave us two free passes to the con."

He's a redhead with a round, freckled face and a rough sense of humor (to put it mildly). We've been friends for a long time, even back when I was still alive, and our friendship had survived me coming back as one of the walking dead. If a friendship can survive that, it can survive anything (though he still makes jokes about the unsightly bullet hole in my forehead).

My caseload at Chambeaux & Deyer Investigations was light at the moment, so I shrugged and agreed to go. I had already been to the Worldwide Horror Convention when it was held in the Quarter last year. I assumed this would be the same sort of thing.

So, that was why the two of us found ourselves in the lobby of the Motel Six Feet Under and Conference Center standing next to two clattery silver-armored cylons from the old *Battlestar Galactica* TV show. They gleamed and hummed, red optical sensors in their helmet visors drifting to and fro.

"CosplayCon security," one said in a vibrating synthetic voice that I could barely understand. He took his helmet off to reveal a young man with dark sweat-plastered hair. "Whew, those things get hot after awhile! Thanks for joining us, but I doubt you guys'll be needed. We don't expect any trouble. Everyone has a good time at the con."

As I looked around the lobby and common areas, I saw Klingons with wicked-looking bat'leths, masked ninjas with curved swords, *Star Wars* stormtroopers with heavy blasters, *Lord of the Rings* orcs with large battle-axes.

"How could there possibly be trouble?" I asked. "Nothing looks harmful at all."

"All the weapons are peace-bonded," said the cylon. When I gave him a blank look and McGoo didn't seem to recognize the term from his extensive Wikipedia research, the cylon security guard said, "Zip-tied. Everything's strapped down so the bladed weapons are perfectly safe. And of course the blasters are just molded resin props. The Jedi lightsabers are neon tubes." The cylon put his helmet back on and told us in his monotone robotic voice, "Have fun—and stay in character," then marched off with a clatter of silver armor.

Tables had been set up in the hall with volunteer staff doing their best to register attendees. This was the first year of CosplayCon in the Unnatural Quarter, and they were glad for the added attraction of real monster attendees as well as cosplayers.

A banner over the registration area proclaimed "We are all someone else inside!" and the program book cover said, "Find your inner YOU!" as if this was a therapy session. Maybe it was—costume therapy.

At the motel front desk, a lone vampire clerk shook his head at all the costumes. He muttered, "Bunch of weirdos," then went back to a magazine he was reading. I didn't see why costumed fans were any weirder than the socially acceptable sports fans who put Viking helmets or cheese wedges on their heads.

Normally on a slow Saturday I might have walked around the Quarter with Sheyenne, or helped Robin finish paperwork on cases. Like any workaholic, I had "fun" by doing my job—solving cases and helping clients. It was my reason for living, in a loose definition of the term.

Over the past decade since their reappearances, unnaturals tended to gather in this section of the city where they were accepted, where they felt right at home. But they still had problems, just like anyone else. While most unnaturals lived perfectly normal everyday lives, some were criminals; others wanted a divorce; others needed to find lost family members. A detective working in the Quarter had the same sort of cases as a mundane detective on the outside, but the clientele was a little stranger.

Back when I was living, and trying to *make* a living, I'd partnered up with a young firebrand lawyer, and I had a good run, a successful business, before I was killed. But, as I said, I *like* doing what I do. So when I came back from the dead, I just got back to work.

In the Unnatural Quarter, being a zombie is no handicap to being a detective, though I insist on maintaining my physical appearance, bathing regularly, going for scheduled top-offs at the embalming parlor, even seeing to it that I receive my monthly maintenance spell. I won't let myself turn into one of those slobbering, shuffling embarrassments that make polite society turn up their noses at zombies.

I'm accustomed to seeing monsters in my everyday life, but I had to admit these costumes were amazing, even a little intimidating, when I started to think about the obsessive time and effort the fans had put into making them.

A squad of white-armored *Star Wars* stormtroopers marched past, representing the 501st Legion, led by an impressive black-caped and wheezing Darth Vader impersonator.

A group of Klingons had taken over the motel's woefully inadequate coffee shop and sat around the tables, pounding fists and demanding more coffee. They grew louder and more unruly by the minute, while a harried-looking mummy waitress tried her best to serve them.

A drunk furry fan was coming on to a full-furred werewolf busboy, who didn't know how to react to all the unwarranted and unwanted attention.

"See, told you this would be fun, Shamble," McGoo said. "Look over there, it's the Doctor. How many can you name?"

I looked around, but only saw a random assortment of eccentric-looking men. "Who?"

McGoo rolled his eyes. "Let's not get into the Abbott and Costello routine. Dr. Who. The first one there with short dark hair—he's the David Tennant Doctor. And the one with the scarf—you gotta recognize *him*—it's a Tom Baker lookalike, probably the most classic Dr. Who. And the one with the bow tie—Matt Smith."

Even after all this time, I was surprised to learn something new about my friend. "I didn't know you were a fanboy, McGoo."

"Not to this extent," he said, gesturing around. "But I've got a TV, and I am culturally aware."

One tall beanpole fan peered over the crowd, trying to reach the information table. Finally he gave up and just yelled, "What time is Van Helsing going to be on stage?" Some of the vampire attendees booed.

"Five o'clock in the main ballroom," yelled an unseen person from behind the desk.

Four skinny guys in clinging red shirts from classic *Star Trek* walked by, and someone yelled in mock panic, "Look out, it's redshirts!" I couldn't see why they posed any kind of threat; in fact, the tight shirts emphasized how scrawny their arms and chests were. If that was the kind of security available to Captain Kirk and crew, no wonder the old show got canceled after only three seasons.

For my own part, I wore my usual sports jacket with crudely stitched-up bullet holes and my fedora—it's my trademark, and what PI would be without one? McGoo wore his blue beat-cop uniform, and everyone seemed to think he was playing a part from an old police show. Several fans came up with very clever guesses from obscure programs that I hadn't heard of in years. One fan marched up with a sneer, poked a finger at McGoo's chest, and said, "T.J. Hooker—not Shatner's best," then walked away without waiting for a response.

Suddenly, we heard yelling from the mezzanine open area and the sounds of a growing altercation. McGoo glanced at me. "This is what we're here for, Shamble. Come on."

We ran up the stairs (and I use the term "ran" loosely, since my joints are stiff enough that it takes me a while to get up to speed). A group of rowdy Klingons yelled, "*Star Trek* is better!" One heavyset Klingon woman had the loudest voice of all.

Across the room, the 501st stormtroopers, who had made an uneasy alliance with costumed Jedi Knights and Mandalorian bounty hunters, took offense. "*Star Wars* is better!"

"*Star Trek*!" insisted the Klingons.

"No, *Star Wars*!" The intellectual debate continued in that fashion for a few more exchanges before the groups ran forward and clashed in an all-out brawl. The Klingons struggled to draw their bat'leths against the peacebonding ties. The stormtroopers punched and pummeled with a clatter of white plastic armor. The Jedi Knights lit their fluorescent-tube lightsabers, but were careful not to damage them.

Before McGoo and I could break up the fight, the group of redshirts rushed into the fray, trying to drive the combatants apart. Eventually, the Klingons brushed themselves off and the 501sters adjusted their body armor. Somehow, the only ones genuinely battered, bruised, and injured in the fight were the redshirts.

"You're right, McGoo. This is fun." I smiled.

Wandering about to get the lay of the con, we walked past large and small panel rooms, costuming workshops, and autograph tables featuring bit actors from long-canceled programs. One large room hosted a "robot smash" where model-builders pitted a remote-controlled R2D2 against a more ominous-looking Dalek. The two machines clashed, with the Dalek crying in a synthesized voice, "Annihilate, Annihilate!" while R2D2 responded with a series of incomprehensible but clearly rude beeps and squeals.

Primarily, though, people wanted to show off their outfits (or lack thereof, in the case of some of the very scantily clad barbarian princesses).

A hard-faced Asian woman wearing a COSTUME JUDGE badge blocked my way. As she ran her critical gaze up and down my appearance, she looked as if she'd had her sense of humor surgically removed. In an officious voice, she said, "I've seen one or two of you already at the con, but your costume isn't up to snuff." She clucked her tongue, then tugged on the front of my sport jacket. "Wrong number of bullet holes on the left. That exit wound in your forehead is at least a centimeter off. And that makeup is terrible. It should be blended more."

"But I'm the real one," I said. "I *am* Dan Chambeaux."

She rolled her eyes. "Right, keep telling yourself that. Getting into character is important, but you have to take the costume seriously, too. After a decade as a cosplayer, trust me I know what I'm talking about. If you're going to be a zombie detective, at least do it right." She walked off muttering.

Loud enough to slice through the background noise came a bloodcurdling scream—and not the good kind of bloodcurdling scream. We hurried toward the source, as did all the other attendees, as if the shriek somehow signaled free beer for everyone.

McGoo and I shoved our way toward a small second-floor panel room, but a crowd had already clogged the door. We tried to jostle people aside, but they reacted as if we were just fellow costumers. So, we got more aggressive and finally made it through the door.

A stormtrooper lay sprawled on his back on the floor—with a wooden stake protruding from his chest. It had been pounded right through the white armor plate.

A burly Klingon stood over him, raising both hands. His bronze skin was flushed and his mouth drawn back in panic. "I just found him like that!"

A young woman in the back of the room—a motel employee holding a pitcher of water for the next panel—screamed again for good measure, although her first scream had already accomplished whatever a scream could do.

By now, all the formerly brawling *Star Wars* and *Star Trek* fans had made their way to the crime scene. The man in the Vader suit came huffing up behind them all, gasping with real exertion that was louder than the sound of his respirator voice box. The stormtroopers reeled when they saw their murdered comrade. One of the troopers looked through the open door and cried out, "Oh, no! It's TK-9399!"

I asked, "You can tell that just at a glance?"

The helmet turned toward me. "Of course, look at the red shoulder pauldron. It's very distinctive. That's TK-9399 all right."

"Yes, I suppose it is." I turned and called out, "Is there a doctor in the house?" The David Tennant, Matt Smith, and Tom Baker Whos arrived, drawing sonic screwdrivers and looking eager to help. I revised my shout. "Somebody call an ambulance."

McGoo drove the spectators away. "Out of the way, all of you. This is a crime scene."

"I didn't do it!" yelled the Klingon, unable to tear his gaze from the body on the floor. "I didn't touch him!"

McGoo turned to him. "I'm Officer Toby McGoohan from the UQPD. I need to ask you some questions. What's your name?"

The Klingon composed himself and said proudly, "I am Ach-gLokh Heqht!"

McGoo had drawn a pad from his pocket, poised to take down the information, but didn't know how to spell it. "Is that a name, or are you coughing up phlegm?"

"That is how I got my name!"

"Ach-gLokh Heqht didn't do it!" claimed a loud and busty Klingon woman. "I was with him at the time."

"No you weren't," I said. "I saw you in the altercation up on the mezzanine just a few minutes ago."

"You would call me a liar?" The Klingon female strode forward as if she meant to tear my limbs off.

I've already been through having a limb torn off, though, and found it unpleasant. I backed away, trying to be calm. "Just stating a fact, ma'am. It won't do for an alibi."

The Klingons regrouped and tried to come up with something else. McGoo and I bent over the staked stormtrooper.

"Take his bucket off," called one of the troopers in a sad voice. It took me a minute to realize that he meant the helmet.

McGoo shook his head. "Nothing gets removed until the Coroner examines him."

"What if he's not entirely dead?" I asked. "Never can tell these days."

Though it went against normal police procedure, McGoo couldn't argue with that. "Right, Shamble. Better make sure." He and I carefully lifted off the victim's helmet without disturbing any other part of the armor.

Then we discovered an even greater surprise. The dead stormtrooper TK-9399 was a vampire.

2

The ambulance and the Coroner's wagon arrived together with a dueling set of screeching their tires in the motel's designated "Coroner" and "Ambulance" parking spot. (The two spots saw frequent use.)

McGoo had called for UQPD backup, and now half a dozen uniformed officers swarmed through the Motel Six Feet Under and Conference Center … which was even more confusing because some of the cosplayers wore similar—some might say better executed—uniforms, including one dressed up as the T-1000 from *Terminator 2*.

The Klingons had commandeered the coffee shop again, where they demanded goblets of warm bloodwine to celebrate the life of TK-9399, whose soul had now gone off to some place called Sto-vo-kor … which sparked a lively discussion as to whether *Star Wars* fans could even go to Sto-vo-kor, or if that was exclusively limited to the *Star Trek* franchise.

McGoo and I went to the Con-Ops room, just off the registration area. We met the pot-bellied and balding con chairman named Phil

Somerstein. He looked bleary-eyed, harried, and overworked with management details. The murder of one of the CosplayCon attendees seemed just one more hassle he had to deal with.

McGoo said, "This is an active investigation, Mr. Somerstein. I'm going to have to impose a lockdown. The murderer is likely still in the motel, and until we've had a chance to talk to everybody, we'll need your help in insuring that all of your attendees stay put."

Somerstein wiped a sweaty palm across a sweaty forehead. "Officer McGoohan, you don't understand—this is *con weekend.* Nobody's leaving the motel, with or without a lockdown."

The elevator chimed, and the doors slid open to reveal two uniformed trolls from the Coroner's office. They wheeled a gurney on which rested the zipped-up body bag. They had placed TK-9399's white bucket on his chest like a memorial, and as they rolled the gurney past, the other 501sters stood in a solemn honor guard, their heads bowed. Darth Vader also hung his helmet, flicking off the respirator in a sign of respect.

One of the stormtroopers shook his white helmet. "He never stopped trooping."

The crime-scene techs had swarmed in with their kits, taking the necessary photos, although many of them spent too much time taking additional photos of sexy Xenas and Wonder Womans (Wonder Women?) who posed for the shots. The police detectives conducted interviews. Off in a quiet area they were taking statements from a Batman and an Indiana Jones.

McGoo looked overwhelmed already. "I may need your help with this, Shamble."

"The cases don't solve themselves," I said. "And you did promise me this would be fun." I was already starting to formulate a plan.

Ach-gLokh Heqht was the obvious suspect, and I've been a detective long enough to know that the obvious suspect usually isn't the guilty one in the end. Besides, if all these cosplayers were really into their characters, why would a Klingon kill someone by pounding a wooden stake through the chest? TK-9399 was a vampire, however, so the murderer's options had been limited. Still, I would have expected a Klingon to, say, decapitate him with a bat'leth and stuff his mouth full of garlic. Then I realized the white bucket would have posed a challenge to the garlic follow-up....

"I can help," said a cheery voice. "It's what I do."

I turned, and faced myself—or at least a reasonable facsimile of me. He extended his hand. "Dan Shamble, Zombie PI."

I was taken aback—he had the fedora, the bullet hole in his forehead (though shifted a centimeter closer to center than mine was), and his skin was pallid. His sport jacket had prominent stitched-up holes. His facial features even bore a strong resemblance to mine. "You dressed up as me?"

"It's an honor to meet you, Mr. Shamble. I've read all your books."

"They're not actually my books," I said. "Someone else writes them, and they're just loosely based on my actual cases." In fact, I found it embarrassing that Howard Phillips Publishing kept releasing comedic horror mysteries that featured the cases of a fictitious zombie detective, based on me. "Just as long as you remember that I'm the real one." I paused to consider. "I'll call *you* Fanble."

He seemed disappointed. "But I have to believe I'm the real Dan Shamble. It's cosplay. I'm in character. Cosplay means you *are* that character, not just dressed like him. It's all about finding the real *me* inside."

"Right. I saw the program book."

McGoo looked from Fanble to me and back to Fanble again. "Usually one Shamble's enough, but we have a lot of potential witnesses and a lot of potential suspects." He raised an eyebrow, as if about to give a test. "Hey, Fanble, have you heard this one? A skeleton walks into a bar, says to the bartender, 'Give me a beer … and a mop!'"

Fanble managed to stay in character by not laughing any more than I did. McGoo has an unfortunate repertoire of bad jokes.

McGoo shook his head. "Yeah, Shamble, he's just like you." He started off down the hall. "Let me talk to the crime-scene techs to see what they found."

I nodded. "Meanwhile, I'll go meet with the stormtroopers, learn more about the victim."

"We're on it, McGoo," said Fanble. "The cases don't solve themselves."

3

After TK-9399 had been hauled away in a body bag, CosplayCon got right back into swing as if nothing had happened. The attendees waited all year for this event, and they worked on their costumes with obsessive attention to detail. They weren't going to let a simple thing like a murder ruin their fun.

I didn't know what to think about Fanble. He seemed earnest and more serious about being "me" than I was. He took great care to imitate my movements, my mannerisms. It was like having my own portable 3D mirror walking alongside me. I decided to accept the help, though. Two heads are better than one when trying to solve a case.

The 501st troopers were nowhere to be found. I looked around, frustrated. "How do you hide a bunch of fans in identical white armor or a tall man in a Darth Vader suit?"

Fanble responded, "It's our job to find out. We are detectives, after all."

As we walked down the hall, other con attendees gave admiring glances and complimented us on our realistic costumes. When I assessed Fanble again, I realized that the bullet hole in his forehead was in the correct spot after all. I must not have noticed it before. We looked like twins.

But the grin on his face made him appear immature and idiotic. Did I really look like that? "Don't smile so much," I said. "It's out of character." He immediately resumed a stern "I'm a PI and I'm at work" expression.

A young man impersonating Edward from *Twilight*—who didn't look like any real vampire I had ever met in the Quarter—asked us if we knew when and where Van Helsing would be giving his talk. Fanble gave him the Crown Ballroom number, then asked if "Edward" knew where we could find the 501st members. I wouldn't have expected a character from *Twilight* to pay much attention to *Star Wars* personnel, but the imitation sparkler directed us to an unused panel room that the stormtroopers had commandeered.

Fanble and I looked at each other. "Do you think they're discussing the case? Maybe working out a retaliation against the Klingons?" he asked.

"Maybe they're holding some kind of memorial for TK-9399," I said. We found the door and pulled it open without knocking. In detective school I was taught that it's best to surprise your suspects.

The surprise wasn't exactly what I'd intended, though, because we came upon a group of half-undressed stormtroopers. Definitely not something I'd ever intended to see.

"Oh, excuse us," I said.

Fanble added in a gruff, no-nonsense voice, "We're investigating the murder of a Mr. TK-9399."

The troopers had taken off their helmets and shucked out of their white resin armor. They stood around in skin-tight body gloves while they adjusted boots, butt plates, greaves, and shin plates.

"Come on in, but close the door," said the troop leader, who identified himself as TK-6370. "We've got an important troop in an hour, lots of exposure, lots of attention. We wanted to check our kits."

"I'm sorry about your fallen trooper," I said. "We're trying to determine who killed him and why."

The stormtroopers grew solemn. "Poor TK-9399. Even after he died and came back as a vampire, nothing changed. I've never seen a fan so dedicated. *Star Wars* is a way of life." That trooper identified himself as TK-7246.

Another trooper, TK-9754, said, "I'm going to miss TK-9399. Sure, he was a fan. Sure, he was a vampire. But he didn't let that change who he was. TK-9399 always used to say '*Star Wars* is my life, and now it's my unlife.'" He picked up a piece of white plastic and turned to the person beside him. "Help me with my codpiece, will you?"

The man in the Darth Vader suit flicked his respirator box on and off, fiddled with the sound effects, then unsnapped a compartment on his wide utility belt to remove a roll of menthol cough drops. "TK-9399 caused quite a stir by trooping as a vampire. He was an activist, even wanted to form an Unnatural Quarter garrison. He tried to round up *Star Wars* fans among the werewolves, mummies and ghosts." He tugged on his black gloves. "He thought it would be cool to have a real ghost Obi-Wan and Anakin, maybe even a troll dressing up as Yoda. TK-9399 didn't expect to cause trouble by expanding the fanbase."

TK-6370 chimed in (and I was proud of myself for remembering the name/number), "*Star Wars* is a pretty diverse universe. Think of the cantina scene, or Jabba's Palace. Gamorreans and Jawas, Twi'Leks and Trandoshans, Gungans, Ithorians—even Chiss and Khomms and Dathomiri."

TK-5794 snorted. "Chiss and Khomms and Dathomiri are from the Expanded Universe. I hear even Disney's dumping those now."

"They still count," insisted TK-6370.

"And don't mention Gungans. I want a Jar-Jar free convention," said another trooper; I was starting to lose track of the numbers.

"Point is, everybody gets along just fine. Why can't vampire fans and human fans share a love of *Star Wars*? But TK-10625 certainly didn't like it. He claimed it was ruining the purity of *Star Wars*, to which we all said, 'Excuse me, *Star Wars Holiday Special*?'"

"And *Greedo* shooting first? Like *that's* pure?" piped up another trooper, to a general groan of assent.

"TK-10625?" I asked, looking around.

"What really bothered TK-10625 was that TK-9399 had to wear a modified stormtrooper suit and armor once he became a vampire. Added sun protection so he could troop out in broad daylight as long as he wanted," said TK-5470. "But TK-10625 said the modifications made the armor an unofficial variant and therefore non-canon."

Several troopers groaned simultaneously. "Let's not get into the canon discussion again."

"But TK-10625 can be a stubborn and angry man. He didn't like the idea of an Unnatural Quarter garrison at all, and he made no secret about that."

Fanble stepped up. "Where is TK-10625 now? We'd like to talk with him."

"Not here," said TK-6370 with a sigh. "Just after the con started, he and TK-9399 got into a huge argument. TK-10625 stormed off, and we haven't seen him since. I was surprised TK-10625 agreed to troop at CosplayCon in the first place."

I glanced at Fanble, then looked at the troopers. "A huge argument? And TK-9399 was murdered right after that?"

The man in the Vader suit frowned. "Sure, but a lot of things happened right around then. I mean, the con was getting into full swing."

TK-5794 glanced at the wall clock. "Time's tight. Better get ready to troop."

TK-6370 nodded. "Happy to help with the investigation, but we've got to be on stage in a few minutes."

Fanble also looked anxious. "I have to go, too, Mr. Shamble."

"It's Chambeaux," I said. "You should know better. What's so important?"

"Van Helsing is about to take the main stage. Who wants to miss that?"

I had intended to miss it, but I let Fanble go, and he dashed off so he could get a good seat. The 501sters finished adjusting their armor components. TK-6370 said, "Buckets on!" and they all donned their helmets. I was now in a room full of identical stormtroopers (although one of them seemed a little short). The man in the Vader suit flicked on his respirator, seated his black helmet in place.

"What is this important troop you're doing?" I asked.

Between gasping breaths, his words garbled by the cough drop, the Vader impersonator said, "We're escorting Van Helsing in the main ballroom."

"And … how can you tell each other apart?"

"We *are* supposed to be clones," said one trooper, and they marched out.

4

Out in the common area, a Heath Ledger version of the Joker was comparing notes with a Cesar Romero version of the Joker as the crowds made their way toward the ballroom, ready for the main event.

Since I was alone for the moment, I took a few minutes to call the office—not because I had any important pending cases, but because I wanted to talk to Sheyenne. "Sorry, Spooky, this was our date day," I said. "You would've enjoyed hanging out at this cosplay convention."

I could picture her ethereal spectral form as she sat at her desk in Chambeaux & Deyer Investigations. She would hold the phone, smiling, her sparkling blue eyes lighting up. "You always take me to interesting places, Beaux."

"Interesting … right. This time a murder's gotten in the way. *Star Wars* fan dressed up in a stormtrooper outfit found dead with a stake through his heart. Turns out he was a vampire. We've got a Klingon as our main witness."

"Oh, another one of those," Sheyenne said. "Are we on the case?"

"I'm here helping McGoo. The motel's on lockdown, but no one seems interested in leaving anyway."

"Let me know if you need our help. Robin and I are here for you."

"I've already picked up an unexpected sidekick," I said, looking around for Fanble, but I didn't see him among the crowds. "I'll explain later."

After I said goodbye to Sheyenne, McGoo came up, red-faced and harried. "I tell you, Shamble, this is turning out to be a full-fledged cluster-frack."

"Cluster-frack? That's a new one."

"From the new *Battlestar Galactica*, Shamble. Get with it." He mopped his forehead. "Ach-gLokh Heqht has gone missing—and the rest of the Klingons aren't talking. He was our only suspect."

"We might have another person of interest." I explained about the internal dispute between TK-9399 and TK-10625.

McGoo looked interested. "All right, let's have a talk with him. Is he with the other stormtroopers?"

"Unfortunately, no. He's gone missing as well."

"How do you lose a Klingon and a stormtrooper in the same day?" McGoo asked, then looked at the chaos of convention-goers and answered his own question.

I said, "I'm going to the main ballroom to see Van Helsing's keynote speech. Since the man's known for killing vampires, it's worth a look."

McGoo, meanwhile, had to get back to the crime scene. The techs had promised some preliminary results.

I entered the Crown Ballroom, where hundreds of chairs were spread out—and everyone was occupied. I worked my way through the costumed and uncostumed fans, many of whom were unnaturals:

curious zombies and werewolves carrying comic book issues and limited-edition action figures. A burly bent-over hunchback clutched a pack of *Magic: The Gathering* cards, and a mummy held a first-edition papyrus scroll covered with hieroglyphics that he claimed was the "real" ashcan version of *Action Comics Issue 0*, available only in Ancient Egypt. He was excited at the prospect of getting it signed by one of the ghost comic creators.

Vampires comprised the majority of the seated audience, apparently having a love-hate relationship with Van Helsing.

Over the ballroom PA system, loud music started playing the thunderous notes of the Imperial March. The audience applauded and booed simultaneously as the costumed Darth Vader strode out from backstage, his black cape flowing, boots pounding on the rickety raised platform, respirator chugging. He reached the podium, lifted his black gloves, and waited for the crowd noise to die down. In his best James Earl Jones impersonation, the suited Vader said, "Some consider me a bad guy, a person who took a walk on the dark side of the Force and enjoyed it. But I did get better in the end."

Several fans in the audience grumbled. I couldn't tell if they disliked his original villainy or his epiphany.

"My exploits are nothing, however, compared to the man I'm about to introduce. The greatest villain known to monsters … the bloodiest serial killer in all of vampire history."

The crowd grew more raucous. They screamed, yelled, and hissed. The vampires in the audience rose to their feet, shaking their fists.

"CosplayCon is proud to present our special guest: For one day only—Honest Abe Van Helsing!"

Vader turned and extended an arm in a dramatic gesture to the curtains at stage left. The vamps screamed and roared, then werewolves joined in, and finally everyone in the audience shared in the hate.

With a clatter of plastic armor, the stormtroopers marched in as an honor guard around a man in a trenchcoat and floppy hat. He had a narrow face, long dark hair, stubbly beard. I wasn't familiar with this incarnation of the character, but he seemed to exude predatory evil and bloodlust. His eyes were close-set and blazing.

When Vader yielded the podium to the guest of honor, Van Helsing just stood there in silence, spreading his glare across the audience and basking in the anger he provoked. "Thank you for the warm welcome. It makes my blood boil, seeing all of you disgusting creatures out there. You think you're safe. You think CosplayCon is harmless fun."

A ghost in the audience yelled, "Boo!"

Van Helsing parted his trenchcoat like a lecherous flasher to show dozens of sharp wooden stakes tucked into his belt, as well as long knives and a bandolier of garlic bulbs across his chest. "I've only got an hour, so I'll just hit the highlights of my career. Let me reminisce about some of the scumbag bloodsuckers I've slain over the years. Ah, there are so many.... Good times!"

The vampires howled so loudly they sounded like werewolves.

"Dracula was the one I killed most often, but that guy's like a Timex watch—takes a staking and keeps on sucking!" He laughed at his own joke. A few audience members groaned. Van Helsing rattled off his favorite impalements, beheadings, or solar overexposures.

As the crowd grew angrier, I wondered if they remembered that this was just a guy in costume, a fan playing a character. Van Helsing seemed to be really getting into the spirit of his cosplay. *Find your inner YOU!*

Thinking of that, I looked around for Fanble, since he'd been so interested, in the speech, but I couldn't spot him in the packed ballroom. I did see a couple of other Dan Shambles, though not as well executed as Fanble's costume.

Even so, I realized that Fanble's preoccupation with me as an alter ego was nothing more than innocent fun. Van Helsing's role-playing seemed deadly serious. If this guy truly believed his mission was to kill vampires, and if he happened to find a vampire stormtrooper alone in an empty panel room, maybe he wouldn't have been able to resist.

I needed to find out if one of his wooden stakes was missing.

After the hour-long panel was over, the crowd filed out of the ballroom, while a few people rushed the stage to mob Van Helsing with questions and curses. Since I had a few questions of my own, I pushed forward, too. "Excuse me, coming through—zombie detective, coming through! Official business—zombie detective."

When I finally reached the front, fans were pushing program books at Van Helsing for him to autograph while cylon security guards tried to herd people into an organized signing line. When I was within earshot, I introduced myself, which got Van Helsing's attention. Although he had a grudge against vampires, other types of undead didn't knot his undies quite so much. "Are you aware there's been a murder here at the con, Mr. Van Helsing?"

"*Doctor* Van Helsing."

"Whatever." I decided to let him stay in character. "A vampire stormtrooper was murdered with a stake through his heart."

"Murdered?" Van Helsing raised his dark eyebrows. "If he was a vampire, wasn't he already dead? I'd call that house-cleaning, not murder."

The gathered vamps spewed more hatred, but Van Helsing ignored them. He looked me in the eye and said, "Vampires everywhere are fair game—even at a cosplay convention. They'd better watch out."

His comment was greeted by more venomous ire … yet somehow his autographing line got even longer.

5

The initial report from the crime-scene techs did not contain any good news. McGoo let out a sigh. "Whenever I have a case like this, why can't we just turn up a simple clue and an obvious explanation?"

"Whenever you have a case like *this*? When do you ever have a case like this?"

"When I'm around you, Shamble, more often than not."

The crime-scene techs had dusted the wooden stake from TK-9399's chest, but found no fingerprints. McGoo tried to draw conclusions. "That means it could have been another stormtrooper—they all wear gloves."

"So does the Darth Vader guy," I pointed out, then attempted to remember whether the Klingon Ach-gLokh Heqht had worn gloves as well. "And so do the cylons. And so do half the cosplayers here. And why limit it to that? Many con attendees are unnaturals, and a lot of them don't have fingerprints at all."

"Yeah, I guess the lack of fingerprints doesn't limit the suspect pool by much."

As McGoo and I talked, two full-furred werewolves walked by, laughing and bumping shoulders. Each wore a Jayne hat, an odd-looking orange-and-brown stocking cap that looked as if it had been knitted by a blind but well-meaning grandmother. The two were immediately adopted by a group of similarly-chapeau'ed Browncoat fans of *Firefly*, the long-ago canceled show from which the style derived. I realized that everyone seemed to be part of one big happy fannish family. All fun and games, until someone gets murdered.

The Motel Six Feet Under was still on lockdown, with uniformed police officers at all doors, but the attendees didn't seem distressed, or even interested in leaving. As McGoo and I contemplated our next step, Fanble strutted up, looking as if he had just won some kind of costume contest. "I got a break in the case," he said.

McGoo looked at me. "How did he figure it out before you?"

Fanble adjusted the fedora. "Never underestimate Dan Shamble, Zombie PI. I had a hunch and, getting into character, I convinced the con chairman to let me see the registration records. He thought I was you." He nodded toward me, then continued his summary. "I discovered that Ach-gLokh Heqht and TK-10625 both registered under the same street name! They're the same person in real life."

McGoo looked at me. "Now that's unexpected."

Fanble nodded again. "Indeed. Crossover fandom doesn't typically happen."

I said, "The Klingon and the stormtrooper were our two most likely suspects. If they're the same person, then it sounds like a slam-dunk." I grudgingly added, "Good work, Fanble."

Fanble grinned before he remembered to get back into character. "The cases don't solve themselves."

"So what's his real name?" McGoo asked.

Fanble showed great pride as he revealed the identity of our likely perpetrator. "John Doe."

Just knowing the suspect's name didn't help much, though. We had no idea what John Doe really looked like, not that anyone really "looked like" themselves at CosplayCon. *Find your Inner YOU!*

If Ach-gLokh Heqht/TK-10625 knew he was wanted for detailed questioning, however, maybe he would hole up where he wouldn't be seen.

"Let's check with the front desk and get his room number," I suggested. "We might find some clues there."

The desk clerk stood behind the front counter, using it as a protective barricade against the costumed fans. McGoo meant business as he strode up and flashed his badge. "UQPD. I need you to let me into a room."

To show that I meant business, too, I held out my official private investigator's ID card. "Zombie detective. I'm with him."

Fanble flashed a fake ID, which, I had to admit, looked pretty good. "Zombie Detective II, Cosplay Edition. I'm with them."

The motel desk clerk, a rabbity little vampire who looked as if he currently regretted his choice of employment, fluttered his hands, mumbled, and turned the computer screen toward him. "And what name is it under?"

"John Doe," McGoo said.

The desk manager keyed it in. "Yes, we do have a John Doe. He's in room 1013. May I see your search warrant?"

McGoo smiled benignly at the officious request. "It's a … welfare check, not a search. We have information that someone may be injured."

"Oh dear, of course! I'll make you a duplicate key."

The three of us waited for an elevator. And waited. And waited. Each elevator stopped at every single floor. The doors finally opened at lobby level to disgorge a throng of cosplayers.

McGoo waved his badge and said, "Police business, we're commandeering this elevator." I pushed the button for 10, and we began to ride upward … but of course we stopped at every floor on the way up. Soon the elevator was jammed with imaginary characters. It was a relief to get off on the tenth floor.

McGoo pounded on the door of John Doe's room. "Police! Open up." When we received no response, he slipped the magnetic card into the key slot and opened the door. "Okay, we're coming in." Before entering, McGoo drew his revolver, and I pulled out my .38.

I was surprised when Fanble also pulled out an identical .38. "Is that real?"

"Part of the costume, for that added bit of realism."

McGoo frowned. "Shouldn't it be peace-bonded, like they said?"

He looked too much like me when he responded, "It would be if they knew about it."

Together, we entered John Doe's hotel room. The shades were drawn. A suitcase was open on the luggage rack. Clothes lay strewn around the floor and furniture, but the room was silent.

"Looks like nobody's home," McGoo said.

"Records showed that only one person checked in here." I glanced at all the clothes.

"Fans often share a room at cons to save money," said Fanble, picking up a long Dr. Who scarf draped over the back of a chair. "Maybe John Doe is more than one person."

McGoo bent over to inspect a half-open black suitcase that contained all the components of stormtrooper armor. "There's not enough normal stuff here, though. Only one suitcase of street clothes."

I found a complete Klingon outfit tossed roughly in the corner. Behind the chair, McGoo was startled to come face to face with a polished silvery cylon suit.

Fanble was amazed. "You know, we never did see any of those characters together at the same time."

"How could you tell?"McGoo went into the bathroom and studied the vanity counter—saw only one toothbrush and a set of basic toiletries. "No makeup here, no prosthetics or wigs. How did he manage that whole turtle head for his Klingon outfit, or the mop of hair for Dr. Who?"

As I went to the closet, I felt a sense of dread. Normally in the Unnatural Quarter you might find skeletons in any random closet, but this time I found something else. When I slid the door aside, I saw the complete Van Helsing outfit hanging there—the trenchcoat, the bandolier of garlic bulbs, the floppy hat, the belt loaded with wooden stakes.

And yes indeed, one of the stakes was missing.

6

TK-9399 had somehow made himself a target for either Ach-gLokh Heqht, or TK-10625, or Van Helsing. An intersection of motives. And if the killer had an entirely flexible murderous intent, then CosplayCon was full of potential victims.

We had to find John Doe—and soon. And among hundreds of disguises.

Fanble had had the bright idea to cross-check the registrations, discovering that the various suspect characters were all under the same street name. I had the equally brilliant idea of flipping that around: we could look up any registrations submitted by "John Doe" and find out what other characters he intended to play. Since we'd already found the Klingon, stormtrooper, Dr. Who, and cylon outfits discarded in the hotel room, John Doe had to be wandering around the con dressed as someone or something else.

As precious seconds ticked away, McGoo, Fanble, and I waited for the interminable elevator. Each time the doors opened, the car was going up, not down. Finally, when another upbound elevator opened on Floor 10, two of the costumed fans motioned us in anyway. "Dude," said a *Star Trek* redshirt, "you have to go *up* to go *down*."

So we rode the elevator up to Floor 14, then back down to the lobby (again, stopping at every floor). When we reached the lobby, McGoo bolted out, and the two of us zombie detectives—both the fake one and the real one—followed him to the con registration desk.

CosplayCon was in full swing, with attendees preparing for the evening's big masquerade, though I couldn't see how an official "masquerade" was any different from the rest of the day here. Natural and unnatural fans were grinning. Werewolves got their pictures taken with Wolverines and a too-scrawny-looking Thor.

We had a case to solve. I could enjoy the con after we captured the murderer.

The registration desk wasn't busy this time of day, since everyone already had their badges and set about to enjoy the convention (at least those who hadn't been murdered or were considered suspects). No one was going in or out of the Motel Six Feet Under because of the lockdown.

A woman sat behind the information table, happily knitting, while a forlorn cat sat in a zipped-up pet carrier beside her. The woman looked up. "How may I help you?"

"We need to cross-reference your database," McGoo said. "One of the con attendees, Mr. John Doe, registered as several different cosplay characters. We need to know the full list so we can track him down."

She frowned and set down her knitting close to the cat carrier; inside, the feline batted at the sidewalls, trying to catch the yarn. "Our computers are down right now, but fortunately, we rely on a more efficient analog system." She pulled out a large plastic recipe box full of colored index cards. "I have every one of the attendees listed here. I can look up your John Doe and pull out his entries."

I let out a sigh of relief. "How long is that going to take?"

"As long as it takes. I'll flip through the cards and pull them out."

"Aren't they organized alphabetically?" Fanble asked.

"No, chronologically. By date of registration." She began flipping through the cards one at a time, starting at the front. While we waited, I looked at the large banner at the doorway: "We Are All Someone Else Inside!"

Right, I thought. *And one of the people here is a murderer.*

A group of rowdy Klingons stormed through the lobby, chasing after a Captain Jack Sparrow who had insulted them somehow. A Mandalorian Boba Fett bounty hunter sneered at a colorful figure of Kenny from *South Park*, saying, "He's no good to me dead."

I picked up a spare program book at the registration desk. "Find Your Inner YOU!" Killing time, I flipped through the program listings. McGoo fidgeted, waiting.

Fanble seemed optimistic. "We're on the verge of solving this case, I know it—and I'm proud that I could help. Is there any better way of getting in character?" He grinned, then remembered his serious expression again. I had to admit, he was doing a decent job.

The registrar's fingers must have been nimble from her knitting. She flipped through all the cards quickly, pulling out every one that listed John Doe. "That's all of them."

McGoo, Fanble, and I turned as she spread the cards as if they came from a Tarot deck. "All these were submitted at different times, all registered to a John Doe. He's a very ambitious costumer." She flipped one down. "Klingon, name of Ach-gLokh Heqht." I was impressed by how well she pronounced the name.

"501st stormtrooper, designated TK-10625. And a Dr. Who—Tom Baker Incarnation—oh, we have several of those here at the con." She kept flipping down cards.

"Old series cylon, toaster variety." She pursued her lips. "Hmm. Honest Abe Van Helsing … one or two of those at the con as well, but he claims to be the real one." She rolled her eyes, "Don't they all? And …" She held up the last card, squinting down at it. "This is strange … he's also dressed as Dan Shamble, Zombie PI."

McGoo looked at me. "What's that all about?"

A cold dread rose within me as I turned to look at Fanble. "You?"

Startled, Fanble raised his hands. His fedora was askew. "No, not me! How could think it was me? It was one of those other guys!" He shook his head as if having a seizure. "That was someone else! They were all someone else!"

"But you're the one who called attention to John Doe in the first place," I said, though I liked to think I would have figured it out myself sooner or later. "If you're the murderer, why would you put us on the trail?"

"Because that's what Dan Shamble would do."

McGoo pulled out his handcuffs, crouched, and prepared for a fight.

Fanble lurched away. His shoulders jittered, his arms flapped. His bullet-ridden sport jacket whipped about as he thrashed. His face blurred like melted putty, fuzzing, reshifting. He shook his head. "No, not me! Gotta stay in character … all the voices in my head!" He clapped both hands to his temples, knocking off the fedora. "Too many personalities. So many expectations!" His features shifted, twisted.

After the cosmic upheaval of the Big Uneasy, just about every form of legendary creature had returned to the world, from basic garden-variety vampires, werewolves, et cetera, to the more exotic mythical beings, even including Santa Claus. After all my years of investigating in the Quarter, I was beyond being surprised when I figured it out. "You're a shape-shifter."

"That would explain all the different characters," McGoo said. "John Doe, you are under arrest on suspicion of the murder of TK-9399."

Fanble backed away, still twisting and writhing. Somehow, he found the energy within himself to snap back into character so that his features looked just like mine again. He reached inside his sport jacket and drew his .38—which I suspected was very real.

The con chairman, Phil Somerstein, ran forward with an angry and annoyed look on his face. "Hey! That's not properly peacebonded!"

A large number of cosplay fans had gathered in the main lobby, many in costume, everyone excited for the impending masquerade. They gasped to see Fanble wave his gun. He pointed the .38 at me again.

I took a chance, though. I saw how determined Fanble was, how hard he worked. His features were so eerily similar to mine it was like confronting myself in the mirror. Holding my hands up, trying to calm him, I stepped closer.

Fanble yelled, "Don't come any closer. I'll shoot!"

"I've been shot plenty of times."

Then the shape-shifter swung the gun toward the fans in the crowd. "Then I'll shoot *them*."

I took another step forward. "But if you're truly in character, as me, then you know I'd never shoot innocent people. Not humans, not unnaturals."

The crowd grew thicker around the tableau, redshirts, numerous incarnations of Dr. Who, Klingons, stormtroopers, cylons, Jedi Knights, Browncoats, Visitors, and countless anime, superhero, and videogame characters, even another faux Van Helsing, whose costume was much less impressive than the one I had seen on stage—the costume John Doe had worn.

And it wasn't just the cosplayers. The unnatural attendees from the Quarter were also caught in the crowd: real vampires, werewolves, even the dedicated mummy fan with his hieroglyphic Issue 0 *Action Comics* ashcan edition.

Fanble's .38 wavered. He swung it around the gathered crowd, then seemed to sulk like a marionette with the strings cut. "You're right—Dan Shamble, Zombie PI would never do something like that." He dropped the .38 on the floor, then shucked the sport jacket, stomped on the fedora—and his features began to morph in an extravagant transformation.

As the flaccid flesh, skull, and facial features reorganized themselves, Fanble shifted through Tom Baker, then into a burly Klingon, thrashed about, and finally settled on a powerful and murderous character, someone who would not hesitate to harm innocent fans: Van Helsing—Honest Abe, ruthless vampire serial killer. His eyes flashed, his dark hair writhed. He drew his lips back to expose his teeth in a glare. "I'll kill you all!"

But despite his facial features, he didn't have his full costume, didn't have his tools or props.

Before McGoo and I could bolt forward to seize him, though, my doppelganger lunged toward the crowd like a quarterback in a game. The fans yelled, trying to scramble away.

Then I saw where he was headed. Van Helsing leaped toward the other Van Helsing cosplayer, knocking him to the ground and ripping at the wooden stakes thrust into his belt. He drew back, holding up one of the sharp projectiles.

Trying to get away, the vampires in the crowd screamed, "Watch out! He's got a stake!"

Van Helsing's hands blurred as if they were rapid-fire crossbows. He hurled his sharp projectiles at random into the crowd, and somehow every stake struck and injured a *Star Trek* redshirt, all of whom dropped to the ground, bleeding.

Drawing my own .38, I yelled at McGoo. "As Van Helsing at least he's *human*. We can take him down."

Realizing his vulnerability as a human, Van Helsing blurred and took on a different form, sprouting fur and massive muscles. His face elongated into a fang-filled canine muzzle and he became a powerful bull werewolf.

I hesitated before I fired, but McGoo didn't. He drew one of his two service revolvers. "I'll just wing him," he said.

McGoo's shot struck him in the shoulder, which flung the shape-shifter backward to the floor of the lobby. He thrashed about like an earthworm on a hotplate.

"It's just a flesh wound. I was careful—Nothing to worry about."

The shape-shifter didn't react as if it were a minor injury, though. He wailed and spasmed, clearly dying.

"What did you hit him with, McGoo?" I asked.

"Uh-oh. Looks like John Doe picked the wrong cosplay creature this time." He looked down at his service revolver. "This is the one loaded with silver bullets in case I get in a shootout against unnaturals."

The shape-shifter moaned and jittered, shed his werewolf persona, and lay twitching—a formless thing like a store mannequin whose features had melted away, gasping out of a round toothless mouth.

He said something, and I bent close, still feeling a certain connection to the man—to the *being*—who had known and imitated me so well. John Doe gasped, "I couldn't stand the pressure … I just wanted to be somebody … to be *everybody*."

With a last writhing rattle, the shape-shifter lost even its featureless humanoid form and dissolved into a puddle of organic goo that seeped into the StainGuard carpet of the motel lobby.

I stood next to McGoo, and he shook his head. "I didn't mean to kill him. Now there'll be a lot of paperwork." He sighed. "I can honestly say I've never seen a shape-shifter before."

I turned to him. "How would you ever know if you had?"

The cylon con security guards came forward to help wrap up, and McGoo decided there was no further need for a lockdown. I realized that it was a good thing McGoo had coaxed me here in the first place.

I felt sorry for Fanble. He had been so earnest, wanting to be the best "me" he could be. I often wondered who I really was inside, just an undead guy who liked to solve cases—was that enough? I had a wonderful (if ectoplasmic) girlfriend in Sheyenne, a great partner in Robin, a true friend in McGoo. I didn't have a need to be anybody else. Zombie detective suited me just fine.

Phil Somerstein announced that the CosplayCon Masquerade would take place in fifteen minutes, on schedule. He called out, "Photo opportunities in the side hall."

McGoo looked at me, adjusted his cap, and I adjusted my fedora. Both of us had to remain in character, of course. "I told you this would be fun, Shamble. Thanks for your help solving the case."

"It's what I do," I said. Maybe I'd call Sheyenne after all. She might enjoy this with me. The event ran all weekend.

As people passed, Phil Somerstein handed out pre-registration cards for next year's CosplayCon. Almost everybody took one.

So did I.

BEWARE OF DOG

1

The snarling whirlwind of fur struck a quiet drinking establishment in the Unnatural Quarter just after happy hour. Rampaging destructive hairy beasts weren't all that unusual in the Quarter, however—especially on a Saturday night.

I wasn't there in person, since my traditional watering hole is the Goblin Tavern, but witnesses described a tornado of claws and teeth. Luckily none of the patrons—neither monsters nor humans—were injured in the howling and smashing, but the New Deadwood Saloon was going to need a complete makeover (which it had needed for a long time anyway).

Sheyenne heard about the incident on the police scanner, and only a few minutes later Officer Toby McGoohan called me to the scene. "Hey, Shamble, I could use your help."

A bar disturbance didn't seem like something that would require the services of a zombie private investigator, but McGoo is my Best Human Friend, and friends help each other out. "I'll be right there."

I tugged my fedora over the bullet hole in the center of my forehead (the formerly fatal wound that had left me a *zombie* detective instead of a regular detective) and donned my sport jacket with the prominently stitched-up bullet holes across the front. After tucking my .38 in its holster, I gave Sheyenne an air kiss (about all I could do with a ghost) and headed off to the New Deadwood Saloon.

The place had batwing doors and an Old West feel—not surprising since the proprietor claimed to be the ghost of Wild Bill Hickok and could produce photo ID to prove it (complete with an olde tyme black-and-white photo on his driver's license). Fake or not, he was a nice enough ghost with big handlebar mustache, leather vest, and bad ectoplasmic teeth from chewing too much ectoplasmic tobacco.

The proprietor had opened up the saloon shortly after the Big Uneasy, and, claiming to have mellowed over time as the world settled down, he now preferred to be called Mild Bill.

Now, standing outside the saloon and looking at all the destruction the hairy whirlwind had caused, the ghost put his hands on his hips. "Golly."

The wooden siding had been raked to splinters, windows smashed, one of the batwing doors ripped off its hinges, and the sign over the door knocked askew so that it dangled on one bent nail. The painted letters said NEW DEADWOOD SALON, with an extra "O" added by hand to correct the embarrassing typo in the last word.

McGoo was already there in his beat cop uniform, notepad out, jotting down the reports of several witnesses: a half-unraveled mummy who looked as if he had tangled with the wild hairy beast, but on closer inspection I saw that he was just naturally disheveled; a dapper vampire, whose tuxedo vest was mis-buttoned by one and who looked as if he had imbibed too much Type AB negative mixed with Scotch; and a befuddled-looking human tourist in a golf cap who had obviously followed the wrong directions from his GPS.

McGoo looked up at me and tipped his blue policeman's cap. "I already called it in, Shamble. A code 10623A, Monster on the Loose (Hairy Variety)."

I inspected the claw marks on the torn wooden siding, pulled out a few tufts of fur wedged in the cracks. "Nobody saw what it really was?"

"No, siree," said Mild Bill. "The thing was moving so fast—it tore up the place then ran off howling. Came in here like one of those Tasmanian devils you see in the nature documentaries."

"You mean in the cartoons," I said.

"Yeah, the animated documentaries. I watch them all the time. Somebody better catch it and put it on a leash."

McGoo pocketed his notebook. "We're on it, Mild Bill. It's not really my jurisdiction, but in the UQPD, the lines between animal control and law enforcement are a little fuzzy."

"Yup, that thing was fuzzy all right." The cowboy ghost looked at the damaged façade of his establishment. "Shoot, I've needed to get a new sign for years. You can't imagine how much ribbing I get for the Deadwood *Salon*. Next time I'll check the work before I hang the sign."

McGoo was clearly done with everything he could do here. "Can you help me out, Shamble? We better catch this thing before it causes any more damage."

He knew I'd agree. "Sure thing, McGoo. The cases don't solve themselves."

2

The monster shouldn't have been hard to track down, since a rampaging furball on the loose tends to draw attention. But no one saw the beast for the rest of the night.

Sometimes, though, an obvious lead walks right through the front door.

Next morning, I was in my office, looking over the files Sheyenne had put on my desk, while Robin met with clients in her office.

Robin is on a crusade to see that unnaturals receive justice, but despite the exotic clientele most of our cases actually turn out to be pretty mundane. This morning, she met with a bickering ghost couple who wanted an easy, no-fault divorce. Robin intended to file on the basis that the "till death do us part" vow set a quantifiable time limit on the contract, and therefore made the marriage of two ghosts no longer binding. I could tell from their squabbling—which Sheyenne and I heard even through Robin's closed door—that nothing about the divorce would be simple.

And then a real-life legend barged into our offices. He was a burly werewolf with thick dark fur starting to turn gray at the temples and around the muzzle. He wore a dark, shabby-looking suit and a thin black tie, something a government agent might wear, or a police detective.

Or a retired police detective.

Or a retired legendary, rogue cop who had become a folk hero in the Unnatural Quarter.

I had seen his furry face on the news, on a poster in the UQ Police Department precinct house, even on action figures and comics. It took me a moment to recognize him, then another moment to get over my surprise.

I lurched out of my office, embarrassed that acted like one of those stumbling zombies rather than the well-preserved one I prided myself in being. I extended my cold hand. "You're Hairy Harry!"

He bristled. "Yes, I am, punk." His clawed hands clenched into fists, and his muscles bulged in his suit, but then the low growl faded in his throat. "I don't like attention, especially after the … incident." Hairy Harry had left the police force under the shadow of scandal, something terrible about the death of his rookie human partner, but I didn't know the details. "I'm retired now, keep a low profile. Just want a normal life—but they won't leave me alone."

Beautiful Sheyenne levitated from behind her desk. "Could I get you something to drink, Mr. Harry? Coffee, tea, soda?"

"Got any bourbon?"

"Afraid not," I said. "I'm a beer man myself, and I do my drinking outside of the office."

Hairy Harry's bristly eyebrows rose. "What kind of private investigator doesn't have a bottle stashed in his desk drawer?"

"A zombie private investigator," I said. "How can I help you?"

"I came to you, Mr. Shamble, because you're a legend yourself—I figured you must be good with all those books about your cases."

"*Based on* my cases," I said, keeping my tone even. "Fictionalized."

"Right," growled Hairy Harry. "Most of the stories about me were fictionalized, too. Didn't stop people from believing them. Right now I need a detective, and even a zombie will do." The restless werewolf cop prowled around the reception area. "My pet hellhound is on the loose, and I need to get him back before somebody gets hurt."

Thinking of the snarling furry beast that had wrecked the New Deadwood Saloon, I thought that was a definite possibility.

Sheyenne said, "What's the hellhound's name?"

"Lucky," said Hairy Harry. "It's an ugly world out there full of punks and dirtbags. He must be lost and lonely." His glowing yellow eyes focused on me. "I want you to find him, Mr. Shamble. I'll pay whatever it takes—just remember I'm on a cop's pension."

"We can work out payment plans," said Sheyenne, who was always business minded.

"Do you think Lucky just ran off?" I asked.

Hairy Harry seemed offended. "A loyal dog like Lucky? He's my guard hellhound. I suspect foul play. Come to my house and have a look at the crime scene. His doggy door was jimmied open—some sadistic pervert nabbed him."

3

Hairy Harry lived in an old, quiet residential neighborhood with a lot of old, quiet, residential neighbors. His house was a modest brick rancher with aluminum awnings over the windows, shrubs that needed trimming, a small lawn that was mowed under duress, and a flowerbed that seemed to grow only dirt. I couldn't imagine a larger-than-life rogue cop planting petunias … pushing up daisies was more likely. The back yard was surrounded by a chain-link fence, probably a place for the dog to run.

The werewolf cop's mood hadn't improved since he reported his stolen hellhound. On the way over to his house, I thought Harry might regale me with his exploits as a tough vigilante officer with a sixth sense for sniffing out guilt and "Jack Bauering" a confession out of a quivering suspect. What I'd heard through the rumor mill was surely exaggerated, but as I rode beside the feral, furry werewolf, I could imagine it wouldn't take much to nudge him into violence.

We went up the front walk, and he used a set of keys to work the locks on his front door—four deadbolts, as well as the lock on the regular knob. "Can't be too secure."

I noticed the large BEWARE OF DOG sign on the garage door, another one taped in the front window, and a third one on a stake pounded into the lawn.

"I made a lot of enemies when I was a cop, plenty of punks gunning for me with silver bullets. I've kept a low profile for years—

I'm done with law enforcement. But a lot of the creeps I put away are just getting out on parole. Damn pussy liberal justice system! They should've all been fried in the electric chair, just because."

Instinctively, I avoided talking about politics or judicial leniency with him, although Robin would have jumped into the debate.

He swung open the thoroughly unlocked door and marched inside, letting me follow. Inside the dim house I could smell the musky scent of damp fur—either Lucky the hellhound, or maybe it was just an old werewolf smell. As he entered the front hall, Harry's shoulders sagged. "I always expect Lucky to come barking and yipping and slobbering all over me, but now the house just feels empty."

I could sense the obvious weight of guilt in Hairy Harry. I doubted he felt bad about all the criminals he'd put away, most of whom had confessed (though many were scarred for life after the experience). "Nice house, Mr. Harry," I said. I feel it's often good to start an investigation with an inane comment.

"It's just Hairy. I stopped being a Mister when I stopped being a cop … after I lost my partner." Shuddering, he hung his head, and his tongue lolled out.

I wanted to ask him about the tragedy, but Hairy wasn't a warm and fuzzy sort of guy. More like prickly fuzzy.

On the mantel in the living room, I saw a large spiked dog collar as big as a basketball hoop. The bristling points were each as long as a sacrificial dagger, and a shamrock nametag dangled from the center. "Is that Lucky's collar?"

"Wow, your detective skills are impressive," he said with a sarcastic edge in his voice.

Trying to imagine the size of the beast based on the diameter of the collar, I thought the New Deadwood Saloon had gotten lucky, and I said as much. The werewolf growled again and slumped in a tattered plaid reclining chair. "I used to drink at that saloon, me and my partner, Amy … though she wasn't old enough to drink. Mild Bill carries good sarsaparilla. Amy really liked it." His claws dug into the fabric arms of the recliner. "But that's all behind me now. I'm just a retired guy who wants a quiet life. Can't a man sit at home with his dog, do the crossword puzzle, watch the shopping channels and laugh at the stupid stuff people buy?"

"Did you have a routine with your hellhound? Did you take him to a dog park, walk him down the street where other people might have seen him?"

"Everybody loved Lucky and he loved everybody—didn't make him a very good guard dog, I suppose. I had an appointment to take him to the vet for some minor surgery, but now he's out there, all alone." His claws shredded the arms of the chair. "And *I'm* all alone. I need Lucky! I got him after … after what happened to Amy. I don't know what I'd do without my dog."

"What happened to your partner?" I asked, then quickly added, "just in case it has something to do with your missing hellhound."

"I was three days from retirement when it happened," Hairy said with a distant look in his yellow eyes. "And Amy was a perky human rookie, almost to her twenty-first birthday, and she'd just gotten engaged to be married. Had everything to live for … until we got into a bad patch, and I failed her."

He snapped his jaws shut, and he turned to glower at me. "That's got nothing to do with Lucky!" He sprang out of his reclining chair. "Let me show you his back doggy door." He strode through the kitchen to the back door, half of which had been replaced with a hinged trap door for a large dog to exit into the fenced yard. The doggy-door hinges had been removed, though, and the panel hung askew.

"What were you doing when Lucky went missing?" I asked.

"I was asleep in my reclining chair, self-medicated with a fifth of bourbon. It's the only way I can chase the demons away, the only way I can sleep. But when Lucky's here, I feel safe—and now I'm not safe. In a world where a hellhound guard dog can get stolen, how can anyone ever feel safe?"

On creaking knees, I bent down to look at the hinges, saw what looked like a smudge of tiny fingers near where the swinging door had been detached. I looked outside in the back yard, saw the four-foot-high chain-link fence that could never contain a large hellhound. "So, Lucky was well trained then?"

"Such a good dog." Harry slid the hanging trapdoor aside. "Some bastards slipped in and stole my Lucky." Rage seemed to boil out of him, and he slashed the air with his claws, but then he deflated. "Find him for me, Mr. Shamble. Before it's too late." He led me back to the front door. "I just might go rogue again."

I remembered the posters in the UQPD: the bristling werewolf cop with his enormous .44 Magnum filled with silver bullets. For the dognapper's sake, I had to keep Hairy Harry from becoming a vigilante.

I started formulating a plan in my mind. I would check the animal shelter just in case someone had brought in a stray hellhound, and the veterinary clinic where Lucky had been scheduled for surgery. Sheyenne could print up LOST HELLHOUND flyers and post them all around the Quarter.

As we stepped onto the porch, though, the werewolf snarled. I saw three figures two feet tall scuttling out of the shrubbery and dashing across the grass. Gremlins. Deceptively cute and innocuous-looking critters, not quite the same as the "don't feed after midnight" variety. These were landbound, not the type to sabotage airplane engines, although gremlins had been known to wreak havoc on unattended lawnmowers.

Hairy Harry bared his fangs and roared. "Get off my lawn!" The gremlins scuttled away in a blur, and I left, convinced that I definitely did not want to see Hairy Harry angry.

4

The first place to look for a lost dog—even a ferocious hellhound—was in the Unnatural Quarter animal shelter. It was a long shot, but I wanted to cover all the bases. Besides, Robin liked to look at the puppies.

Robin has a personality that makes her want to help the downtrodden, including oppressed monsters, anyone caught up in unfortunate circumstances; by extension, her compassion embraces lost animals as well. She's a beautiful young African American woman with a hard persistence when she's on a case and a dazzling smile when she's about to win. She believes in the Law and Justice (complete with the capital letters), but the real world doesn't always operate the way her law books describe, and sometimes I have to bend the rules to shield her.

The UQ animal shelter was a cacophony of yips and growls, snarls, hisses, subsonic vibrations, and smells that made even my deadened zombie olfactory senses ready to shut down in dismay. Robin was stoic about it, though.

The animal shelter had specific sections for reptiles, felines, canines, large arachnids, and "other." Some rooms were barricaded with heavy steel doors and reinforced bars; others had special spell wardings. A lost hellhound, no matter how large and ferocious, would've been the least of the animal shelter's worries.

Robin and I made our way to a reception desk staffed by a young human woman with round glasses, long straight hair parted in the middle, and a Summer of Love hippy peasant dress. She seemed unfazed as a skeletal gray-skinned woman (and I use the term loosely) harangued her. "Puppies!" she shrieked. "I want all of your puppies."

The woman's spiky black hair looked like a startled porcupine on top of her head. Her face was gaunt, all angles sharp, and her skin had a zombie-like pallor; I could tell she was a lich, but from the way she treated the kindly receptionist girl, I could think of at least two other lich homophones that would have been appropriate.

"I'm sorry, Miss De Ville, but we have no puppies available this morning," said the receptionist.

Robin and I both recognized the name at once. Coupe De Ville, a well-known undead socialite, who threw gala fundraisers that attracted the Unnatural Quarter's snootiest investors and philanthropists, though no one could quite identify which charities were the beneficiaries of such largesse. I suspected Coupe De Ville simply pocketed the donations to finance her lavish lifestyle.

Now, she pointed a long claw-like finger at the receptionist. "How can an animal shelter not have any puppies?" She swirled and glared at us as if we would join her in the shouting.

"Sorry, they're all gone as of late last night," said the poor receptionist.

Robin stepped up. "We were looking for puppies as well."

"Actually," I interrupted, "I'm trying to track down a missing hellhound that's been on the rampage." I withdrew one of our Chambeaux & Deyer Investigations business cards. "I'm Dan Shamble, Zombie PI. This is my partner Robin Deyer."

"I was here first!" shrieked Coupe De Ville in a voice that would've made a chalkboard cringe in anticipation of sharp fingernails.

"And you've been here for quite some time," said the mild-mannered receptionist.

The socialite's white fur coat was comprised of countless small swatches of fur—from skinned lab rats, hundreds of them. Robin frowned. "Are those lab rat pelts?"

Coupe De Ville whirled on her, flashing sharp white teeth in what she might have considered a smile. "*My* lab rats, from *my* laboratory." She said the word with an emphasis on BORE. "They displeased me."

"And why do you want all the puppies?" I asked. She didn't seem like a cuddly pet owner.

"For various purposes," said Coupe De Ville before turning back to the receptionist. "Now, why don't you have any puppies?" Her sharp claws scraped on the countertop leaving long gouges.

"We … lost them all," the young woman admitted. "An animal activist group broke in last night, opened the cages, and set them free. They're gone."

Coupe De Ville looked furious.

"What about a hellhound?" I said. "Did you have any hellhounds?"

The receptionist looked at her records. "No, not in at least six weeks. Hellhounds tend to be adopted quickly."

"Which animal activist group?" Robin asked. "I know several of them."

"It was GETA. They left their calling card, graffiti scrawled a foot off the ground."

I couldn't figure out how the height of the graffiti letters would be significant, but Robin turned to me and explained. "GETA—Gremlins for the Ethical Treatment of Animals. Little guys that cause a lot of havoc."

"Gremlins as a species like to sabotage things," I said.

Coupe De Ville snarled. "Little terrorists."

Robin continued, "At first they were called GET-U, which stood for Gremlins for the Ethical Treatment of Unnatural-Animals. They liked the sound of the acronym, but in the end they disliked the hyphenate compound. Gremlins are inclined to sabotage, but they're sticklers for grammar and punctuation."

In a huff, Coupe De Ville swirled her white lab-rat coat. "Call me when you have more puppies." She stormed out.

I tapped my cold finger on the business card, sliding it closer to the receptionist. "And hellhounds. If you get any lost hellhounds, call me. I have a distraught client who wants his dog back."

5

After hours when I went for my usual beer on my usual bar stool at my usual place, McGoo was already there. He does a lot of business and pondering on that bar stool. During the day he caffeinates himself with sissy-sounding cinnamon lattes from the Transfusion Coffee Shop, and at night he takes the edge off with a pint or two of whatever is on tap at the Goblin Tavern.

Francine, the human bartender, took care of her patrons, most of whom were abuzz about what had happened at the New Deadwood Saloon. They congratulated themselves on choosing a less hazardous watering hole.

"Hey, Shamble," McGoo said, raising his pint. "You know why companies don't let zombies take coffee breaks? Because they have to retrain them afterward!"

So that was how the night was going to start out. It was no better and no worse than the usual. "I may be the butt of your jokes, McGoo, but you're just a butt." I stiffly maneuvered myself onto the bar stool.

I decided the best way to distract him from offering a second joke was to tell him my news. "Got a new client today, McGoo. Hairy Harry hired us to find his missing hellhound."

Officer Toby McGoohan has seen all sorts of things in the Quarter—and I do mean *things*—from resurrected corpses in beauty parlors, to necromancy spells gone wrong, to tentacled monsters in the sewers, and an evil elf trying to drive Santa Claus out of the holiday business. He took all those things in stride, but now I thought his eyes might actually pop out of his skull.

"You mean, *the* Hairy Harry? But he's retired. No one has seen him … since the last time they've seen him. He's a legend. Every cop looks up to him, both naturals and unnaturals. He knows how to put punks in their place, and he doesn't take crap from desk jockeys. Hairy Harry single-handedly busted up dozens of crime rings, even a crime octagon once. He cleaned up the streets of the Unnatural Quarter . . . until it all went south after what happened to his partner." McGoo hung his head. "He was never the same afterward."

I was about to ask more when the Goblin Tavern's door opened and two towering hairy creatures entered. At first I thought they were wookiees, but I knew that was impossible because wookiees aren't real. These two—one with matted brown fur and the other with a mottled gray and white pelt—were a Sasquatch and an Abominable Snowman, respectively. Their heads nearly scraped the ceiling as they walked around the bar tables, holding out a donation bucket and passing out leaflets.

They represented the Bigfoot/Yeti Visibility Society, "Yes We Do Exist!" They passed the patrons in the bar, holding out the change bucket, but no one seemed to notice them; they just continued their conversations. Since I'm soft-hearted (even if it's not a beating heart), I fished out a dollar and dropped it in the bucket. Robin, with her deeply ingrained sense of social justice, would have been proud.

McGoo looked up, startled. "What was that for?"

"A donation for the Bigfoots and Yetis."

He looked around and just glimpsed the two hairy creatures as they walked back out the door. "Oh, I didn't know they existed. I was thinking about what happened to Hairy Harry."

Francine brought me my own beer—I didn't even have to order—and I took a sip. "Tell me about Hairy's partner. He didn't want to talk about it, but I gather that her name was Amy?"

"Yeah, she was a rookie and he was the curmudgeonly old cop. Insisted that he didn't want a partner, that he always worked solo, but his chief stuck him with a young lady fresh out of the Academy, cute as a button. Officer Littlemiss. Hairy Harry never stopped being a curmudgeon, but she grew on him."

"I've seen that movie," I said. "In fact, several dozen of them."

"They were chasing a mummy mobster, Lenny Linens, who made a fortune selling counterfeit monster versions of classic Hummel figurines. Hairy Harry and Officer Littlemiss tracked him to the warehouse where he stored the black-market Hummels. Officer Littlemiss suggested calling for backup, but Hairy wanted none of that. The rookie wanted to use due process and arrest Lenny Linens so he could have a fair trial."

"I can guess how that went over with Hairy Harry."

"You'd guess right," McGoo said. "He didn't want the kid in the line of fire, so he told her to stay put outside while he broke into the warehouse. Hairy stalked the mobster through the warehouse, prowling along the dim aisles."

I felt a sense of dread. "I'll bet Amy didn't stay outside. She went in to help him, right?"

"Yes. I read the full inquiry—every cop does. It was a real cat and mouse. The two of them separate, tracking Lenny Linens—and when the mobster felt cornered, he started shooting. Shattered Hummel figurines everywhere." McGoo shook his head. "But that wasn't the real tragedy. Officer Littlemiss ran to flank the mummy while Hairy Harry bounded along the rows of boxes. Officer Littlemiss cornered Lenny Linens, told him to freeze, identified herself as UQPD.

"From the other side of the stacked boxes, Hairy Harry says all he heard was voices, then a gunshot. He opened fire with his .44 Magnum, blasted craters right through crates of vampire shepherd boy figurines and little werewolf riding hoods and cute baby witches with angel wings. Hairy Harry prided himself on shooting first and not bothering to ask questions later."

My heart was always a dead lump in my chest but now it felt heavier. "He shot Officer Littlemiss, not the crime boss?"

McGoo nodded. "When Harry realized what he'd done, he crashed through the shelves, pounced on Lenny Linens, and unraveled the mummy entirely. At the inquest, he said he was in such a blind rage he didn't even realize what he was doing. You know the rest of the story, Shamble. Big scandal, Harry booted off the force, couldn't live with himself, and just disappeared." McGoo lifted his beer in a silent salute. "We still consider him a hero at the UQPD."

I raised my glass to touch his, but I was already thinking about the case. "And now someone stole his hellhound."

6

The next morning as Robin met again with the divorcing ghost couple, I went to check out the veterinary clinic where Hairy Harry had made an appointment for Lucky. Fortunately, there had been no further incidents of a rampaging, ferocious beast the previous night, but it was only a matter of time. In the Quarter, it's always something.

Dr. Moreau's Veterinary Clinic (Sterilization Specialists) advertised "We serve all species, breeds, and dimensional aspects. Heightened security available upon request." As I approached the entrance, I encountered a small protest—actually it was a regular protest, but with small participants. A group of angry gremlin demonstrators, obviously members of GETA, marched up in front of the clinic. The gremlins looked determined, though with their diminutive size, not very intimidating. They carried signs, waving them in the air so that they came up to my waist, "Neutering is Nuts!" or "Protect Procreation!" or "Stop Spaying!" The gremlin at the end of the parade line carried a sign that said "Allow Alliteration!"

I dodged past them, careful not to trip on the socially-aware gremlins. When they yelled at me for crossing the picket line, I brushed them off. "I don't even own a pet."

"Want a puppy?" asked the gremlin carrying the "Allow Alliteration!" sign.

I wondered if some of the strays unleashed from the animal shelter had followed them back to their secret GETA headquarters. "Not at the moment," I said. "Maybe for the holidays."

I pushed through the door into Dr. Moreau's clinic, a place of stainless steel, reinforced windows, and surgical theaters. As I stepped up to the front desk, the nearest operating theater door swung open and a burly man in a surgical gown and mask strode out. He had rubber gloves covered with green blood. He wore large aviator mirror-shades.

"Mark down another success, Maria," he said. "You can tell Mrs. Johnson that her basilisk is spayed." He lifted his sunglasses. "And yes, these reflective shades work just fine. Good to know."

A surgical assistant in scrubs, with her hair tucked in a surgical cap, opened medicine cabinets and took out vials of antibiotics and de-wormers.

The receptionist marked down the successful surgery before looking up at me. "How may I help you?"

"Zombie PI. I'm here to speak with Dr. Moreau." I flashed my private inspector's badge and glanced at the veterinarian.

"Sure, what do you need?" said the big man. "Are those protesters still cluttering the front door? GETA is a PITA—Pain In The Ass! They don't understand the good work I do here. They want to protect the masculinity and femininity of unnatural animals, but who wants packs running loose? Have you ever seen a demon cat spraying to mark his territory? Or a hellhound in heat?"

I seized my chance. "A hellhound is what I'm here about, Dr. Moreau. Hairy Harry has lost his pet, Lucky, and I'm trying to track down all leads. I understand he had an appointment for some minor surgery here?"

"Oh, that one—I remember!" Moreau scratched his surgical cap. "We had already arranged security for the hellhound."

The surgical assistant finished arranging the bottles of medicine, took a vial of antibiotics, and headed for the operating room door. "I'll go check on the patient, Doctor."

He nodded absently, but just as she swung open the door, he extended his mirrored sunglasses. "Wait—"

But she didn't hear him in time. She walked into the operating theater where the freshly spayed basilisk was recovering. We heard a loud, terrified cry that turned into a bloodcurdling scream, then silence.

Moreau hung his head. "I lose more assistants that way. When dealing with unnatural animals, you have to take precautions."

I was worried. "Should we go investigate?"

"No, she's already turned to stone. Sometimes they get better, sometimes not. Nothing we can do." He turned to the receptionist. "Can we install more mirrors in the operating theater as a security precaution?" Then he glanced back at me. "Now where was I?"

"The hellhound, Lucky?"

"Yes, we were all ready, but Hairy Harry never showed up, so I canceled the appointment. We have a surcharge for that." He adjusted his surgical mask again. "I wish I could help you, Mr. Chambeaux. What's my next appointment, Marie?"

"A nightmare stallion in operating theater two, Doctor," she said. "To be neutered."

"One nightmare gelding coming up." Dr. Moreau took a large pair of bolt cutters hanging on the wall. "If I think of anything, Mr. Chambeaux, I'll call your office." Swinging the heavy tool, he went into the second operating theater.

7

The raging furry terror struck again that night, but instead of attacking a popular drinking establishment, the creature chose an odd target: an abandoned warehouse that had once been a laser-tag arena, "now featuring REAL DEATH RAYS!" The death-ray/laser-tag business had gone belly up though, probably because their clientele perished after only a few visits.

I met McGoo at the scene of the carnage. Claws and teeth had torn open the corrugated metal walls, peeling them aside like an orange. The windows had been shattered. Long silver claw marks looked like extended lightning bolts across the metal walls.

"Must have been the same thing that struck the New Deadwood Saloon," I said.

McGoo nodded. "You sure it's Hairy Harry's hellhound?"

"I can do the math, even though math was never my favorite subject. Any security cameras here?"

He frowned at me. "Who would be watching this place, Shamble? The squatters tore out the cams and sold them for parts a long time ago."

"Squatters? Does that mean there were witnesses?"

"No. They only sleep here during the daytime—a couple of trolls and a werewolf girl with a bad case of the mange. They were out panhandling when it happened."

"How does a wild hellhound just disappear, McGoo? Hairy Harry thinks Lucky was dognapped—but if that's the case, why would it go on random rampages?"

McGoo and I walked around the crime scene. "I put out an APB for a violent furry beast that's prone to ferocious destruction, and our tip line has been flooded. Apparently that's not a specific enough description in the Unnatural Quarter."

I looked up at the dilapidated death-ray sign, tipping my fedora back so I could see better. "An abandoned warehouse? An unlikely target. Why would a hellhound attack here?"

McGoo grinned. "I know something you don't know, Shamble—and if the monster really is Hairy Harry's hellhound, maybe …"

"What?"

"Before this place was a death-ray/laser-tag arena, it used to be a warehouse—a criminal warehouse, owned by a mummy black marketeer. Lenny Linens." He grinned, and I caught on.

"This is the warehouse where Hairy Harry had his shootout? Where Officer Littlemiss was killed?"

"Win a prize every time, Shamble. Now that's a connection you can work with."

8

I felt guilty about laughing over someone else's misfortune, but it really *was* funny. Besides, Coupe De Ville had done very little to endear herself to the general public.

Walking on legs that were as thin and brittle as mummified sticks and adorned with sagging fishnet stockings, she emerged from a fancy boutique on Hyde Avenue. That's not an area I normally frequent, since uptown is too highbrow for me and most of my clients, but Hairy Harry and I were walking down the street when it happened.

The socialite lich wore an overabundance of unnatural bling: gaudy amulets, and necklaces of heavy moonstones that looked like eyeballs. She was haughty in her patchwork white coat made of lab rat fur, surrounded by a miasmic cloud of perfume from sampling every possible aroma in the boutique.

Coupe De Ville lifted her sharp chin as if she meant to cut the air and yelled for a taxi. Her severe face turned into a rictus of disappointment when a cab did not instantly appear.

That was when the rambunctious and militant GETA gremlins rushed out of an alley, yelling, "Puppy parasite!" and "Pet predator!" They carried plastic Solo cups full of scarlet paint, which they hurled at her. Several gouts only reached the lich's knobby knees, but one gremlin was exuberant enough to splash paint all over her rat fur coat. Then the gremlins dropped their empty plastic cups and raced away, laughing and cackling.

Under the best of circumstances, Coupe De Ville's voice was enough to make my skin crawl, and now her scream was enough to shatter glass. Fortunately, the jewelry stores and high-end perfume shops on Hyde Street all had reinforced windows to protect against burglars and, as it turned out, shrieking liches.

As she stood horrified at the red paint splattered over her, it really wasn't terribly funny—I know that. But Hairy Harry started chuffing first, and I couldn't help myself. It was good to hear the rogue werewolf cop laugh for a change.

He had been so forlorn and distraught ever since he came into our offices in search of Lucky. Sick of waiting around for news, he had begged to accompany me this morning as I walked the streets in search of clues. As a police detective himself back in the day, Hairy Harry knew the technique of "investigation by wandering around."

After last night's attack on the former black market Hummel warehouse, a place that had so many dark memories for him, Hairy Harry was in even worse shape. His lupine eyes were bloodshot, as if he'd been crying through the night as well as howling at the moon. He shook his shaggy head. "It's more important than ever that we find Lucky—before someone gets hurt." He suggested we go uptown. "Some rich types might want a purebred hellhound. You never know." I think he just wanted company.

Hairy was a rumpled, no-nonsense sort of werewolf, who, in his years of being a tough cop, had seen it all, then gone back for a second look.

He wasn't much for conversation, though. We had been walking along in companionable guy silence, not bothering to look in the store windows. I would have enjoyed the stroll more if Sheyenne were with me, even though we couldn't afford most of the things in stores like these. I couldn't pronounce most of the brand names, much less identify the type of merchandise they specialized in. I admit it, I'm not entirely sure I even know the definition of "couture."

Laughing at Coupe De Ville's misfortune didn't prevent Hairy Harry's cop instincts from kicking in. A werewolf cop can retire but he'll always be a werewolf cop. I controlled my laughter, too, as my detective instincts kicked in as well. "I want to talk to those gremlins. I keep bumping into GETA at every step in my investigation. They may be involved in the disappearance of your hellhound."

Hairy Harry's hackles rose. "Let's go."

Coupe De Ville was still waving her clawed hands in the air, looking in revulsion at the red paint that splattered her rat fur coat. She was in such a horrifying state that even well-meaning people didn't dare go closer.

I called out as Hairy Harry and I dashed past her after the gremlins. "We'll try to catch them, ma'am."

"But who's going to help *me*?" she wailed.

I gestured toward the curious onlookers. "They will." The crowd bolted as soon as I made my suggestion.

The werewolf cop put his nose to the ground, sniffed the discarded plastic cups, then loped off. "I'm on the scent."

I did my best to keep up with him. Fortunately, I stay in good shape, regularly working out at the All-Day/All-Nite Fitness Center, shambling along on their treadmills.

The paint-hurling gremlins were small but they could run fast on their little legs. Gremlins like to throw a wrench in the works, then dash away before they get caught—but they weren't used to being tracked by a werewolf cop and a relentless zombie detective (although my contribution to the pursuit was definitely secondary).

We never caught sight of the fleeing gremlins as they dodged from street to street, but Hairy Harry kept after them. As he ran along bent over and nose to the ground, his jeans slid down, letting me glimpse too much of his big hairy butt crack—not something I wanted to see, but I'd seen many horrific things before.

The werewolf cop slowed, sniffing harder. "We're close." He turned down a narrow side street, passed several unmarked tenement doors, then stopped at a low delivery door with a side mailbox labeled "GETA Secret Headquarters."

"This is the place," I said.

Hairy Harry snarled sarcastically. "You really are a detective."

As we approached, I drew my .38 just in case there was trouble. The werewolf gave my weapon a scornful glance, then withdrew his much more impressive .44 Magnum. Hairy Harry smashed the door with a clawed hand, then charged in. "Got you, little bastards!"

Inside GETA headquarters, the gremlins scrambled about in a panic. Several were washing up, changing clothes. They recoiled in alarm as we burst in, and several raised their hands in surrender upon seeing Hairy Harry's gun, which was about the size of their smallest member. One gremlin raised Neutering is Nuts! picket sign defensively, though a .44 Magnum blast would cut right through it as easily as it cut through a wall of monster figurines and one rookie cop.

I pointed my much-less-impressive pistol at them. "Caught you red-handed." Two of the quivering gremlins did indeed have red hands from spilled paint. "We saw you dump that on Coupe De Ville."

"She's an evil lich," said one of the gremlins.

"She wears fur coats. Think of all those poor lab rats," another gremlin said. "And she keeps adopting puppies. I think she eats them. They're never seen again."

The gremlin peeked out from behind her Neutering is Nuts! sign. "And she's not a nice person at all."

"GETA defends animals of all kinds, even the nasty ones," said the leader of the group. "We're here to stop the torture and the experimentation."

Another gremlin said, "And the neutering." His voice cracked in a high falsetto.

From behind a door in the back of the GETA secret headquarters, we heard a scuffle, a yipping sound, then muffled shouts.

Hairy Harry perked up his tufted ears. "That sounds like Lucky!" There was no stopping him as he boiled forward. Snarling, he swung his Magnum and blasted open the door to the back room. He didn't even bother to try the knob. The 44-caliber bullet blew the knob, the hasp, and half the door into shrapnel, then Harry smashed it inward.

Wooden steps led down to a basement, from which we heard excited barking and yipping.

I swung my .38 at the embarrassed and frightened GETA members in the main room, then I followed Harry down into the cellar of the secret headquarters. The basement was a wreck—not a chamber of horrors, but cluttered and ransacked … as if it had been torn apart.

Hairy Harry immediately spotted the dog. "Lucky!"

Lucky really was just a puppy, about the size of a young German Shepherd. The small hellhound bounded forward, delighted to see his master. In his jaws, the puppy held a terrified and squirming gremlin by the scruff of the neck. The captured gremlin screamed for mercy, and Lucky dropped him on the cement floor, then bounded forward into Hairy Harry's well-muscled arms.

"I expected him to be a little bigger than that," I said.

"He'll get there," the werewolf growled. "Right now he's just a puppy with plenty of puppy energy." Harry tugged the ears and shook the dog's head back and forth as he cooed in a baby voice, "Isn't that right? Isn't that right?"

Lucky's tail wagged furiously, thumping against the open-frame cellar wall. Bored and rambunctious, the puppy had already ripped out the wadded insulation from the walls, knocked over boxes, spilled debris and laundry. I saw two other gremlins cowering in the corner, as if afraid the hellhound might want to play with them as well.

Lucky licked Hairy Harry's face, and the werewolf started licking him back. I grabbed the shaken gremlin that had been dropped from the puppy's jaws. "Why did you kidnap this dog? What did you mean to do with him?"

"We were saving him!" the gremlin cried.

The other cowering creatures came forward, struggling to find their defiance. "We knew about his appointment at Dr. Moreau's clinic."

"His master was going to have him neutered. That's a majestic hellhound. You can't emasculate a hellhound!"

The puppy barked and bounded toward the cornered creatures as they ran screaming for cover.

"He seems to be quite a handful," I said.

Hairy Harry glared at the gremlins. "And *you* want to handle a full-grown hellhound with too much testosterone? I suffer from the same problem. I love my puppy, and I'm not going to have him go through that."

"Save us," cried the gremlins. "Take the dog!"

Hairy Harry wrapped his big arms around the puppy and pulled him away from the terrified creatures. "Aww, he's just playing. That's what a puppy does. Maybe I should throw one of you across the room and say fetch."

The gremlins screamed and cowered.

"We should take Lucky and go," I said, trying to defuse the situation.

Hairy Harry glared at all of them. "You don't know how much damage you almost caused. Maybe you should try to understand the bond between a werewolf and his dog. I need my puppy."

Hairy Harry made sure his .44 Magnum was tucked in its holster, then he clapped his paws and made the dog follow him up the stairs. I swept my gaze across the cowering gremlins. Since Hairy was too distracted to remember it as he took his hellhound out into the streets, I said, "You just made my day."

9

Later that week, Hairy Harry called me back to his house for a visit. His voice sounded much happier, and his grin showed sharp teeth as he let me inside. "Things are back to normal, Mr. Shamble. Thanks for your help."

"Glad to have another satisfied client," I said. "So, Lucky was unharmed?"

He led me through the house to the back porch. "Yes, though he doesn't think so right now. I just brought him home from his appointment at Dr. Moreau's." He lowered his voice. "Snip, snip."

In the fenced-in yard, Lucky bounded around chasing leaves, although he was befuddled by the plastic cone around his head that prevented him from licking his new testicle stitches.

I thought of the enormous spiked collar on the mantelpiece back inside the house. "I have to ask. That collar is enormous, but Lucky is just a normal sized puppy."

Hairy Harry glanced back at the big spiked ring. "A dog can dream, can't he? Most people think *I'm* larger than life. I wanted my dog to be the same."

I thought I understood.

The werewolf cop leaned against the brick wall. "I feel so much more content now that he's back. Lucky calms me, keeps me at peace, guards me against my nightmares … and all those memories." Hairy Harry hung his head. "Now that I've got Lucky back, the Quarter doesn't have to worry about some infuriated monster wreaking havoc anymore. Lucky's calmed me enough. I can handle the stress now."

I was confused. "Isn't Lucky the one that caused the damage to the old warehouse and the New Deadwood Saloon?"

Hairy Harry blinked his yellow eyes, then chuffed out in laughter. "No—that was me. When I have an episode, sometimes I go a little … crazy. After what happened to Amy, and all the guilt and trauma I went through, I've been diagnosed with severe PTSD. I get flashbacks, panic attacks. They turn me into a wild beast. I can't control it. Lucky's my service dog, assigned to me as my best friend. It's therapy."

"That raging destructive hairy monster was you?" I asked, still trying to wrap my head around it.

"Lucky keeps me centered, calms even the worst flashbacks." On the back porch, he bent over and slapped his knees. "Here, boy! Come here, Lucky!" The hellhound bounded over, wagging his tail from the hindquarters on down. He didn't seem to hold the neutering against Hairy. The dog leaped up, placed his paws on his master's shoulders and slobbered all over his face.

Hairy Harry laughed. The dog let out a yip, and the werewolf responded with a loud howl. When they circled and started to sniff each other's behinds, I decided the case was solved and hurried back to the office.

About the Author

Kevin J. Anderson has published over 125 books, more than fifty of which have been national or international bestsellers. He has written numerous novels in the *Star Wars*, *X-Files*, and *Dune* universes, as well as a unique steampunk fantasy novel, *Clockwork Angels*, based on the concept album by legendary rock group Rush. His original works include the *Saga of Seven Suns* series, the *Terra Incognita* fantasy trilogy, the *Saga of Shadows* trilogy, and his humorous horror series featuring Dan Shamble, Zombie PI. He has edited numerous anthologies, including the Five by Five and Blood Lite series.

Additional Copyright Info

"Stakeout at the Vampire Circus"
First published as a Kensington eBook; first print publication in *Slimy Underbelly* by Kevin J. Anderson, Kensington Books, 2014.

"Road Kill"
First published in eBook form from WordFire Press (2012); first print publication in *Mister October: An Anthology in Memory of Rick Hautala*, vol II, edited by Christopher Golden, Journalstone Books, November 2013.

"Naughty & Nice"
First published in eBook form from WordFire Press (2013); first print publication in *A Fantastic Holiday Season: The Gift of Stories*, edited by Kevin J. Anderson and Keith J. Olexa, WordFire Press, 2014.

"Locked Room"
First published in *In Shambles* anthology, Jesse Duckworth, ed., Harren Press, 2014.

"The Writing on the Wall"
First published in *Dark Discoveries* magazine—Issue #28, JournalStone Publishing, 2014.

"Role Model"
First published in *Fiction River: Fantastic Detectives*, Kristine Kathryn Rusch, ed., WMG Publishing, 2014.

"Beware of Dog"
First published in *Streets of Shadows* anthology, edited by Maurice Broaddus and Jerry Gordon, Alliteration Ink, 2014.

OTHER WORDFIRE TITLES

Our list of other WordFire Press authors and titles is always growing.
To find out more and to see our selection of titles, visit us at:

wordfirepress.com

52312718R00111

Made in the USA
San Bernardino, CA
16 August 2017